THE WEDDING DRESS

This Large Print Book carries the
Seal of Approval of N.A.V.H.

THE WEDDING DRESS

DRESS

Virginia Ellis

Thorndike Press • Waterville, Maine

Copyright © 2002 by Virginia Renfro Ellis

Published in 2002 by arrangement with The Ballantine Publishing Group, a division of Random House, Inc.

Thorndike Press Large Print Women's Fiction Series.

The tree indicium is a trademark of Thorndike Press.

The text of this Large Print edition is unabridged.
Other aspects of the book may vary from the original edition.

Set in 16 pt. Plantin by Liana M. Walker.

Printed in the United States on permanent paper.

Library of Congress Cataloging-in-Publication Data

Ellis, Virginia Renfro.
    The wedding dress / Virginia Ellis.
      p. cm.
    ISBN 0-7862-4705-3 (lg. print : hc : alk. paper)
    1. Women — Southern States — Fiction. 2. Southern States — Fiction. 3. Wedding costume — Fiction.
4. Reconstruction — Fiction. 5. Poor women — Fiction.
6. Sisters — Fiction. 7. Large type books. I. Title.
PS3605.L47 W43 2002b
813′.6—dc21   2002028404

To the women who wait . . .
then stand up and go on

To my friends, colleagues, and cheerleaders:

Sandra Chastain, Pat Von Wie,
Deborah Smith, Debra Dixon,
Nancy Knight, Martha Shields,
Donna Ball, Amelia Renfro,
Nancy Renfro, Vickie Doran,
Andria Bramlett.

And lastly, to my agent, Claudia Cross,
and editor, Shauna Summers — for believing.

Chapter One

October, 1865

The war has been over for six months, yet the dream came again last night. I'd thought it left me, after plaguing me for two years without mercy, then inexplicably stopping. But as I lay motionless in the darkness, alone, eyes wide open, held prisoner by the familiar overwhelming sadness, I remember.

It is my wedding day. And in the dream William stands tall and handsome at my side proudly wearing his lieutenant's uniform of the 24th Virginia. In this welcome glimpse of the past, my William, my husband to be, looks fearsome and beautiful, so alive and in a fever to claim me as wife before going to war. The beloved vision of him breaks my heart. Because I know what comes next. I remember the weary path of this dream well. What comes next is that as I stand there, in front of family and friends — half of Patrick County — on the happiest day of my life, I look down at my beautiful, heirloom wedding dress, the same gown my mother wore to pledge her life to my father, and see that it is covered in blood.

The blood of war and mortal men. Of broken dreams and severed vows.

You see, I am the middle child of three, all of us girls. Our duty, and the best we could do for ourselves and our family was to marry well, have fine, healthy children, be obedient wives, and good Christians. So far, my sisters and I had failed on every count beyond marriage. My elder sister, Victoria, should have married first, but when I met William and fell heels over head in love, my father thought it circumspect to marry us before our passion got out of hand. William's family agreed. So, I was the first to take the vows, to become Lieutenant Mrs. William Lovejoy, wearing my mother's dress.

So much has happened since then.

Victoria did marry, six months after I did. My parents were still with us then and even though our fortunes were slimmer, I believe they were proud of her choice. My sister's husband, James Whitmore, touched our lives only briefly. Of good family, but little wealth, he, too, marched off to defend the South from the Unionists. Very few months after his departure he was reported missing and presumed dead following the battle of Chickamauga. We never heard from him again.

In a way I was luckier than Victoria. I knew what had happened to my William. He'd made arrangements with his men that they should get word to me if something unfortunate occurred and his men honored him by keeping their promise. I received a letter from a Sergeant Tacy saying that William had died on the third of July in Pennsylvania at a place called Gettysburg, serving bravely under General Longstreet. The names and places meant little to me then — Cemetery Ridge and Little Round Top. What meant more was that Sergeant Tacy had written to say my husband's last words had been of me.

And now the dream was back. Why? I had come to terms with fate and the past the best I could through prayer, hard work, and sacrifice. Lying in the dark listening to the mockers and the house sparrows beginning to stir, I couldn't fathom the reason.

Then, I heard a woman weeping.

For one silly moment I thought the sound had originated from me, or was a spectral echo of the nights I had cried myself to sleep. Rising and turning my head, however, helped me find the source. The mournful sobs were coming through the wall, from my younger sister, Claire's room. I lit a lamp and went to investigate.

"What is it, Sweet?" I lowered myself onto the side of Claire's bed and pushed the damp hair out of her eyes. At seventeen years, Claire was already a beauty like our mother, with fair hair and china blue eyes, blooming even in so spare a garden as our small, out-of-the-way plantation, Oak Creek.

Claire pulled away from my comfort and sobbed louder.

"Are you ill?" I was beginning to worry. We were far from any doctor and had precious little money to pay one.

She shook her head and drew in a long steadying breath.

"What is it then?"

"I can't say," she mumbled. "It's too ungrateful. You and Victoria have lost —"

Still in the dark, I persisted. "Victoria and I have what?"

Claire carried on louder then, and I heard the door hinges squeak. Looking up, Victoria met my gaze with a question in her eyes. I shrugged my shoulders as a signal that I didn't know yet. Victoria nodded and closed the door. As we had always done with Claire, I would reason with her first. If I failed, then Victoria would step in. We did the best we could without our mother. After all, we were grown women. Women who would have had children of our own to handle if not for the intervention of the war. And Claire was hardly a child. She herself should have been married by now.

"I'll never marry," Claire practically wailed.

The fact that her thoughts had been so close to my own startled me. "Of course you will," I soothed, saying the obligatory words when the truth was, I had little hope. "You'll meet a handsome gentleman who'll melt your heart." I thought of my own William and felt tears sting my eyes once more. Straightening my shoulders, I blathered on before both of us were wailing into the bedclothes. "Now that the war is over —"

"Now that the war is over, all the men are dead," Claire interrupted angrily. Just as quickly her anger disappeared. She threw herself into my arms. "I'm so sorry! I didn't mean it. I didn't mean to hurt you."

It did hurt, but it wasn't Claire's doing.

I'd learned in hard fashion that wars are fought by the men, but it was the women who must deal with the aftermath. "It's all right, Sweeting. I know." I stopped before telling her she was right, that she probably would become a spinster. In the past, before the war, there would have been formal dinners with dancing, or picnics on the church grounds, many opportunities to meet eligible young men of good family.

The memory of dancing with William under festive lanterns hung in the trees filled my mind and heart. I wanted to close my eyes and breathe deeply to find the sweet perfume of honeysuckle as I had that evening. But winter had come, and William would not dance with me ever again.

The war had changed everything.

The victors were calling it Reconstruction, but I could see little hope that the world we had lost would ever be restored. Good fortune had kept the fighting from our land. That and our utter lack of strategic value. Off the beaten track of the main movements of both armies, we'd only been relieved of some livestock and vegetables by foraging Confederates. Even they had seen fit to leave us one milk cow that had since gone dry, one old horse, Jeremiah, one pregnant sow, and half our chickens. In deference to our men fighting for the cause, I suppose.

Now, however, with the war lost and President Lincoln dead by the hand of what the Federals called "a Southern sympathizer," we had no idea what to expect. We'd be lucky to keep our family land, much less have families and a future of our own. But, just in that moment, I didn't have the heart to crush Claire's hopes. "Let me think on this. If you truly want to marry, I shall find a way."

Claire was silent then and looked at me with all the hope and faith of a child whose sister had never failed her. I knew I had to find a way. I held her until she stopped sniffling and shaking. By that time, red streaks of morning sun lightened the sky and our two remaining roosters were crowing to herald the new day.

I waited until Claire had gone out to the barn to collect eggs before broaching the subject to Victoria. We were in the cookhouse making breakfast. We'd learned to cook for ourselves since we couldn't afford any help these days, and since only the three of us sat down to any meal. The food wasn't always pretty, like our mother had insisted upon, but it was serviceable. I will say, however, that it's much more pleasant to watch someone churn butter than it is to handle the enterprise one's self.

"We must find a match for Claire and get her married," I announced, as if it would be an easy task.

Victoria's competent hands stilled over the biscuit dough on the board and she gazed up at me. "How will we do that?"

"Perhaps we could send her to our cousin down in Savannah." I knew the suggestion was made of air, but said it in any case. We certainly couldn't send her to Richmond, which was closer. We had no kin there and most of the city itself had to be "reconstructed" after being razed by fire.

"With no money and no trousseau? You may as well send her as a beggar." Victoria directed her attention to the dough again and pushed it with some agitation. "Besides, if less than half the men in this county returned from the North, how many do you suppose went home to Savannah?"

"What of Savannah?" Claire's voice sounded lighter than it had in months as she stepped through the door. For a moment she appeared years younger than seventeen and my heart hurt at the beautiful truth of who my sister really was — a young woman full of hopeful potential. It wasn't fair that her future had been snatched from her before she'd had the opportunity to claim it. I pledged my faith once more to give her what she wanted and to help her find her happiness.

"Oh, nothing," I answered and held out my hand for the basket of eggs. "We have a cousin there."

"Could we go and visit?" Claire asked, again seemingly able to divine my thoughts.

"We will see," I replied, shooing her out of my way. "I'm not ready to speak of my plans yet."

For the remainder of the day I worked on a solution. I double-checked our accounts and scoured for any extra money. I silently inventoried the house, room by room, searching for something valuable we hadn't already parted with. In the attic, I opened trunks and poked through dusty castoffs in hopes our parents might have hidden and then forgotten some treasure.

What I found instead, was the gown I had worn at my wedding, packed away between layers of tissue that had turned yellow with time. For a moment I feared that the dress would appear as it had in my dream. I had to work up my courage to pull it free of the trunk. The silk of the gown itself had parted here or there but the color had warmed to a lovely ivory. The beading on the lace appliqués looked newly sewn, and gazing at it somehow brought back my mother's words, "My father had it made for me in Paris." She'd been so proud of this dress, and even prouder that I should wear it. Victoria had worn it as well.

Perhaps we could patch the tears well enough for Claire to use it for her wedding. Or, we could carefully clip the stitches of the appliqués and sell them. After all, beadwork from Paris was scarce in the South in these days. Busily calculating as I looked down at the yards of material so lovingly preserved, I suddenly felt the great crushing weight of all we'd lost in these last four years. To my surprise, I saw a drop of water fall and sink into the silk, then another. I realized I was crying. My legacy from the dress had been a dream of blood and war, the loss of our parents, and an uncertain future. Victoria had faired little better.

No. I pushed the dress back under the tissue. Claire would not wear this gown, nor would we strip the last heirloom of our family bare. My younger sister would have her own dress, her own new beginning. A start without haunting dreams of loss.

I made the announcement that night over supper. "I've decided that Claire shall have a wedding dress."

The silence at the table lasted for a full three beats of my heart before Claire burst out with, "Oh, Julia, really?"

Victoria sat speechless.

I raised a hand in Claire's direction to temper her enthusiasm. "Now we may have to barter for cloth and make the gown ourselves, but you shall have one."

My pronouncement didn't deter her eagerness. She obviously didn't need a new gown from Paris; she was overjoyed at the prospect of having one at all. For a moment, her excitement seemed to burn away the usual shroud of disappointment, if not outright unhappiness, that kept us constant company.

"And then will we go to Savannah?" Claire went on, not particularly worried about the details.

"We'll fashion the dress first, then find you somewhere to wear it," I said, avoiding the opportunity to burst her bubble of happiness. Of course we had no money to go to Savannah. That was one of the clamoring details I was sure Victoria would quiz me about later. I put later out of my mind. It lifted my own careworn heart to see my younger sister with hope in her eyes again. We had gone too long without it.

Victoria waited until Claire had left us to go to her room and dream of her new future before approaching me with serious eyes.

"Do you know what you're about?" she asked. "Why a wedding dress? Claire was unhappy before, but if you get her hopes over the moon, what will happen when there's a bad ending?"

I put down the book I'd been merely holding and met her question head-on. "Of course I don't know what I'm doing. But I'm determined to give one of us a normal life no matter what it takes. Claire feels she has no future. A wedding dress represents hope for a new life, for love and family . . . a kind of enchantment."

"There are women over the entire South missing their men or wanting a husband. Wishing it different won't make it so." Victoria nearly hissed the last words, not out of anger, I knew, but because she wouldn't be the one to hurt Claire with the unpleasant truth of overheard words.

I took her cool hands in mine. "My dear Victoria, it's up to you and me to get some backbone about this. We had our opportunities. . . ." I squeezed her fingers trying to take some of the pain out of the words. "Now we must give Claire hers.

"You love Claire, I know you do," I said. Victoria nodded her agreement. "Beyond that, we've both tried to keep the family going through our losses." Again, she agreed. "When I first thought of finding a match for Claire it was to assuage her pain, but I've come to realize that finding her a future ensures our own. If none of us marry, then it will be the end of our family, of all those who went before. And I, for one, won't let that happen. It's up to us, you and me, and Claire, the last of our family, to ensure it doesn't die."

Victoria had tears in her eyes. I hugged her hard. "You're right," she whispered in my ear. "I'll do whatever you wish."

Honesty struck then. "You first must help me believe we can do this."

Victoria drew away, pulled a patched hanky from the cloth at her bosom and dabbed her eyes. Then she straightened her spine and gazed at me with a new fearsome expression. "We can do this."

Chapter Two

We sold two pairs of our best shoes, our father's old musket cleaning tools, an armload of mama's finest linens, and two of our good laying hens to get the buff-colored calico. There was no silk to be had and anything fancier was beyond our limited means anyway. Mr. Tate at the mercantile kept scratching his head about the purchase, no doubt thinking the widowed Atwater sisters had gone round the bend. Then to Victoria's horror, I announced, "Our sister Claire is getting married."

That shut him up. But on the way home, as our only buggy horse, Jeremiah, plugged along, I had to defend my words.

"It's one thing for us to make fools of ourselves, but to tell Mr. Tate! It'll be over the county in a week. Then what do we do when —"

"You're supposed to help me believe, remember?" I said, quickly. "And if you believe, if we both believe — why, we'd tell folks, wouldn't we? I figured having the entire county believe would help us all."

Victoria had no argument for that queer logic. For most of the ride home she was silent. But then, as we turned onto our own drive, she asked, "What do we say when people ask *who* she's marrying?"

"We'll say he's a brave Virginian on his way back from the conflict. When his duty is finished, he'll be here to collect his lovely bride."

She looked at me closely. "We haven't seen a soldier on this road for months. You haven't truly gone round the bend, have you?"

I raised my chin. "If I have, then I have good reason. We both have good reason. So, if we fail, you and I can pretend to be batty for a year or two and everyone will get past it and forget."

Victoria's smile was only half convincing. "Everyone but Claire."

We began the dress on the last evening of October, a time when the garden had been knocked down by the first frost and our days were less occupied. After giving the sitting room a thorough cleaning, we opened our out-of-date but still serviceable fashion plates, and began plotting. We measured

Claire for a flounce here, a swag there. It was rather fun, actually. Soon the three of us were laughing as though the future truly did hold the promise of a wedding.

But as we spread out the pristine, nearly-white cloth, without mark or stain from the past, our laughter faded. I think we were all struck silent by the possibilities of a new beginning. I held up the scissors.

"Let us put our hearts and our minds to one purpose," I said, feeling as solemn as a devout preacher stepping up to the pulpit. Both my sisters' hands covered mine on our mother's sewing shears and we each said a silent prayer. I knew what Claire's would be — for love and a family. And mine, mine gelled into a fierce determination. We would make this happen, a future for Claire somehow, some way. I put out a silent call for help, to our parents, to our God, even to William.

As I opened my eyes and gazed at my sister Victoria, I was struck by the look of utter peace on her face, so calm and deliberate. I didn't know the content of her prayer but she seemed to have heard the answer, as if we'd already succeeded. Never had I loved my sisters more. With one last squeeze of comfort, we separated our hands and set to work.

We established a pattern of working an hour or two each afternoon. There was no hurry, as we'd decided a spring wedding would be best. Also, we had to guard from making mistakes. Pins were scarce and no extra money could be spared to replace any disastrous wrong cut or misfit. We took our time, Victoria and I doing the lion's share of planning and cutting. Although, in order to lend her moral support, Claire began embroidering the cuffs and sash since we had no lace.

A week after our ceremonious beginning, a rider came up the drive. We speculated as to who it might be for a full twenty minutes. It turned out to be old Mr. Satterwhite from a neighboring farm over ten miles distant. He and his wife had been friends of our parents but we hadn't seen them since our father's funeral. I remembered hearing that his son had come back to his wife and children from the war, but the former soldier had left his right leg somewhere in The Wilderness. His return had not been much help for a farming family.

Mr. Satterwhite looked dusty and seemed rather uncomfortable to be standing in our front yard holding a leather pouch. I was so surprised to see him, I immediately thought to hear bad news.

We gravely invited him into the parlor while Claire took his horse to water. We had little else to offer the animal besides frost-bitten grass. For Mr. Satterwhite, we brewed up some sassafras, having nothing in the way of proper store tea. After enough time had passed to salve our sorely out-of-practice social skills, I asked what he was about.

"My wife has it that your young sister —" he inclined his head toward the front door where he'd last seen Claire "— is about to be married."

A strangled sound come out of Victoria, but I cleared my throat and answered, "Why, yes. We are planning on a wedding in the spring."

For a few seconds, barely more than the blink of an eye, his face seemed to soften. As if he might be thinking back to happier times. Then his frown returned. He put down his teacup and picked up the leather pouch at his feet. "Well, then, she hasn't sent me on a fool's errand." He proceeded to pull a paper-wrapped bundle from the pouch and handed it to Victoria who was closest to him. "She sends her — our well wishes."

"Thank you so —"

26

Victoria's gasp interrupted me. When I turned to see the cause, she had pulled the cord on the bundle and was reverently touching a bolt of white lace and three spools of white silk thread.

"This is so lovely," Victoria said in whispered admiration. She looked up with glistening eyes. "Mr. Satterwhite, we couldn't possibly take this —"

He raised a gnarled hand to stop her, and his mouth twisted into what might have been a smile. "It's little enough. In better times we could do more. My wife has no daughters to see married." His smile faded once again. "And you have no mother for Claire. We would consider it an honor to our good friends, your parents, for you to accept this as a wedding gift."

Stunned by generosity we'd long since done without, I couldn't speak. Luckily, Victoria was in better condition. She immediately thanked him and, by proxy, his wife profusely, asked him to stay for supper, then walked him to the door when he declined. My last vision of him was as he took the reins of his horse from Claire. He bowed over her hand as gallantly as a man half his age and kissed her fingers before congratulating her. Then he mounted his horse and rode away.

Claire was beside herself over the lace. She took it to her room that evening and placed it near her pillow to keep it safe. Hours later, after we'd long since retired, I remained awake, struggling with my duplicity in beginning this whole enterprise with nothing but a wish, when Victoria opened my door.

"Jules?"

She hadn't called me by my childhood name in years, and for some reason the sound sent a shiver through me. "What is it?"

Without a word she came over and squeezed my hand, hard. I felt her trembling. The feeling of dread didn't leave me as she led me from the room. A few moments later we were standing in her room before the window looking east.

"Look," she said, but I didn't need her urging. I could see very well why she'd brought me to her window. "Are they soldiers?" she asked.

I pushed my face closer to the cold glass and stared out at the night. A campfire burned in the distance — over in the direction of the Powder Mill Road. By the glow of the fire, I could see figures walking under the great oak tree near the crossroads. More than a few, but less than a dozen men had camped within a mile of our home. The sight reminded me of the many times during the last four years that I'd seen regiments of soldiers, marching, foraging, tending to the business of war. Now, however, with the battlefields silent, the sight seemed more ominous. Another chill ran through me.

"Should we walk out closer and see who they are?" Victoria asked. As small as she was, she'd been afraid of little in her life. Perhaps it came from being the oldest child or a replica of our father in female form — coal black hair and dark, serious eyes. It took a lot to set her on end.

I gripped her hand tighter. "No. Let's leave them to their business and hope they don't come this way. You go back to bed. I'll sit and watch for awhile."

"I'll bar the doors first," Victoria replied. She left the room without a lamp to go downstairs. In normal times there was little reason to lock the house. But during the war, we'd made a habit to close up to discourage opportunistic robbery or worse. Now we would go back to the old ways. The fire glowed in the distance as I sat down to observe.

I woke up in Victoria's bed. The first hint of dawn had brightened the sky and my valiant sister was sound asleep in the armchair at the window. It had rained during the night making it undoubtedly cold and miserable for the men on the road, but no one had approached the house. We had survived. Now it remained to go out and see what we could find in the way of clues as to who the men might be.

Over a hurried breakfast, Victoria and I explained what we'd seen the night before to Claire. We had no wish to alarm her, but if there were groups of men, or even more unlikely, soldiers about, then we all needed to be on guard. None of us was to stray too far from the house alone and whoever went would carry our father's pistol. We decided that we would take the carryall out together to the campsite and see what we could find.

We found nothing.

After traversing the road and the entire area we believed to be the campsite, the only wheel and horse prints on the rain-washed ground were our own.

"Perhaps they left when the rain began," Claire said.

"Perhaps," I replied but was troubled by one other thing. The men I'd seen had built a sizable fire to keep warm. We'd found no evidence of blackened wood or ashes. The old oak looked as though it had been passed by for years, with not a trace of occupation.

Puzzled, we all slept a bit lighter for the next week. Yet soon, without proof or dire consequence, our good spirits returned and we went back to our routine of working on Claire's gown. One afternoon, as Claire measured pieces of her precious lace for the bodice, I heard her say, "Oh, no," under her breath.

Thinking the lace had met an unhappy fate I jumped. "What happened?"

Claire gave a little laugh. "Oh, nothing. I just realized we don't have any buttons for the back closing." She looked slightly embarrassed. "It's all right. I can pilfer the ones on my last Easter services dress."

"But aren't they pink?" Victoria asked without looking up from her stitchery.

"Pink or white, it doesn't matter," Claire responded with sauce in her tone. "Either way they will undoubtedly keep the dress from falling down."

Victoria smiled and nodded in agreement.

"Undoubtedly."

I thought of the dress up in the attic, the heirloom gown. It had white, silk covered buttons. If we found no others, I would cut them off myself, but I still hoped for a completely new dress for Claire, untainted by the past. Keeping my silence on the matter, I held up the back panel I'd been sewing and sighed. "Well, that's finished. Only ten more panels to go."

"I think we're going along well," Victoria said. "After all, it's only the middle of November."

"Which serves to remind me," I said. "It's time to take that young sow to the Pelton's for smoking or we won't have a Christmas ham. I think tomorrow is as good a day as any if you two will help me coax her into the wagon."

"We don't have to coax," Claire offered. "She'll follow a trail of acorns anywhere. I'll pick up a basketful in the morning."

"Then we could make a day of it," I said. "We can deliver our hopes for Christmas dinner, and stop in town for the other things we need."

Chapter Three

The sow proved a bit more reluctant to board the wagon than the basket of acorns could overcome. We settled on putting a rope around her neck and pulling her firmly up a plank into the bed of the wagon. On the way into town she attempted escape three times. Losing my patience with the entire process, I put Claire and Victoria off in front of the mercantile and drove the two miles out to Pelton's on my own. Just me and the firmly trussed-up sow.

Once I arrived, the transaction didn't take long. The sow was happy to get off the wagon with the older Pelton son. We agreed that I could pick up the smoked meat and sausage at any point beyond ten days. The butchering and smoking would cost one of the hams.

Relieved to be free of my passenger, I boarded the wagon and headed back toward town. The day was cool but clear and the smell of wood smoke brought memories of other, happier times. William had come home from the war on a short furlough in the fall over two years before. He'd been thinner and grimmer but still looked upon me, his wife, with loving eyes. I only wished I'd become with child then, on that visit, because it was the last time I'd seen him in the flesh.

The memory of my terrible dream came back as the wagon creaked along Thomasville Stoneman Road, and I forced my thoughts to the scenery around me. As I gazed ahead, I saw a thin plume of dust rising in the distance, moving toward me. I squinted. It looked like several horsemen with perhaps a wagon following. I continued on, not knowing if I'd be forced to pull off the track to let them pass.

"Now, Jeremiah," I said to our horse. "Who do you suppose that could be?"

Like he'd been listening, Jeremiah suddenly raised his head and pricked his ears. He'd either heard a sound or picked up a scent.

As the distance between me and the unknown travelers closed I could discern several men walking behind the riders. The sight reminded me of the men who'd camped under the oak on Powder Mill Road. And, after issuing a list of rules to Claire and

Victoria about never going out alone, etc., I found myself breaking each of them save the one about Papa's pistol. I reached down near my feet and raised the sack where I'd stored the gun. I might be alone, but I was not without the means to defend myself. Besides, these were probably people I'd known all my life, neighbors, on their way to one place or another on this public road. Nothing to fear.

That's when I noticed they were soldiers. At least a company by the looks of them. The rising dust obscured the color of their uniforms but I caught sight of their colors being carried by one of the horsemen.

Confederate soldiers.

My heart gave a leap as if it would soar out of my bodice. Even Jeremiah seemed a little skittish and he was so old it would take a starving mountain lion intent on dinner to bring him to a gallop. What in Heaven's name was a company of Confederate soldiers doing on this road when General Lee had disbanded the army six months prior? Were they deserters? Partisans continuing the fight?

Without any further options other than astonishment, I directed Jeremiah to the side of the road and pulled up. I took the pistol from the sack and hid it in my skirts before the soldiers were close enough to observe me. Then I waited.

The men were marching quickly — with a destination in mind, certainly. It was a goodly march to Richmond from here, but the city had fallen and most of it burned months before. I straightened my spine and made ready to greet them. But as they drew close, my heart nearly stopped and my throat wouldn't have produced a word under the threat of eternal silence.

The soldiers were mostly gray. Gray uniforms, gray ash in their hair and on their battle-hardened faces. The dusty disturbance in the air seemed to follow them rather than falling away, and they made no sound as they moved. No clinking of canteens or shuffling of boots and hooves. The horses were gaunt and in need of good rest and pasture. I could see that some of the men had wounds, a bandaged head or an arm in a sling. But there was no color of blood, only gray.

The oddest thing, however, and the most difficult part of the vision, as I will call it now, is that the men were all slightly faded, as though their living essence had been bled into the Earth, leaving only the outer shell. And each shell was transparent at the edges. As the men marched, I could occasionally see through a uniform to the trees beyond, through a horse to the man bringing up the rear, like this company of gray soldiers walked half in one world and half in another.

I held my breath at the otherworldly sight of them, but not a single man either glanced at me or acknowledged my presence. One of them seemed to pass right through Jeremiah causing the old horse to nervously sidle away from the ghostly apparition.

Papa's pistol made a thump as it fell to the floor of the wagon, my entire body having gone numb with disbelief. I wasn't truly afraid. Well, not of these soldiers, anyway. It was the manner of seeing them, in broad daylight on a well-traveled road. Was the entire Confederate army still marching in some netherworld, refusing to give up the cause? Or were they caught in a never ending hell because they'd failed to defend their homes and ideals? A new fear clutched my breast. Was my William still grimly marching on a far-off battlefield without even the promise of eternal rest?

I turned quickly, without thinking further and called to them. "Do you know Lt. William Lovejoy of the 24th?"

My voice sounded small and tentative in

my own ears, and it was answered only with silence. As I watched, the dust obscured the last of the group and they faded from view. Stepping back into their own separate world it seemed. Feeling awed, yet foolish at the same time, I retrieved Papa's gun and restored it to the bag. I then picked up Jeremiah's reins, gave them a snap, and headed for town.

On the way there, I began to seriously consider that I had lost, or was in the process of losing, my sanity. First the return of the dream, then the phantom men at the crossroads and now, this unholy specter of ghostly soldiers. I had to tell Victoria my fear, but I didn't relish the chore. Her sanity was beyond question, and she would need to be strong enough for the three of us if I was losing mine.

I reached Stoneman without any further incident and stopped on the edge of the main street to compose myself. I didn't intend to tell Victoria immediately because I didn't want to frighten her and Claire. So, I straightened the pins in my hair, pinched some color into my cheeks and took several deep breaths to prevent myself from hurtling into my sister's arms wild eyed and weeping, which is how I felt inside. Losing a mind, I understood, was serious business. But, it wouldn't happen before we traveled the road home.

Finally, I felt ready. I picked up the reins and said, "Let's go on, Jeremiah."

"Are you all right?" Victoria asked immediately when she saw me.

I was disgusted. So much for my brave outer appearance. I refused to cave in, however. "Why, certainly I'm all right," I answered as I took a bundle from her and set it in the wagon.

Victoria searched my face. "I had the oddest feeling while you were gone. And, remember, you said we shouldn't be traveling alone."

Now if anything, this unsettled me even more. Staid, sensible Victoria was having "feelings." Were we all losing our handle on normal life? Just then Mr. Tate, the proprietor of the mercantile, came out carrying a sack of cornmeal with Claire following behind him. As he hefted it in the wagon, I gave Victoria a warning look. I had to know if my worries had a basis.

"Mr. Tate? Have you by any chance seen any soldiers passing through the county lately?"

Mr. Tate stopped dead still as though he'd heard a gunshot. Then he turned to me like I'd pulled the trigger. "Soldiers?"

After another long look he answered, "You and I know the army's been disbanded. I haven't seen a soldier around here since the end of the summer." His eyes narrowed speculatively, enough to make me wish I'd kept my question to myself. I certainly couldn't explain what *I'd* seen. "Now why would you want to know about —" Then he seemed to notice Claire once more. "Oh, that's right. Miss Claire is waiting for her intended." He turned to her. "I wouldn't think your beau will come back wearing a uniform," he said. "But you be proud of him, just the same. We all done our best. At least that damned lil' General left this county alone." Color rose from his collar up his neck. He nodded awkwardly. "Excuse my language, ladies. Oh, and Miss Claire, remember if you want them buttons you admired in the catalog, you just send me word. I'll order 'em up for you."

After Mr. Tate had inquired if we needed anything else of him, he retreated back into his store.

"What was that about?" Victoria asked as we boarded our wagon.

"Nothing really," I said airily and inclined my head toward Claire's back. Victoria merely nodded. I knew she'd be sorry she'd asked when I told her later, but that couldn't be helped.

On the drive home I did my best to keep a civil conversation in progress.

"Claire, what is this about buttons?" I asked.

Claire's face fell. "I didn't tell Mr. Tate to order them, Julia." She looked as though she might be punished for looking.

"I didn't accuse you of any such thing," I said, giving her knee a pat. "I was only curious at what you picked out."

"Victoria told me it would do no harm to look in the catalog, so I did. And, they had the loveliest pearl buttons that looked so real — as if you had sewn a beautiful necklace down the back of the dress."

"How much were these beautiful buttons?" I asked.

Claire didn't speak at once. "I was only dreaming," she said belatedly.

"They were five dollars for twenty-four," Victoria answered.

I swallowed back any comment that immediately came to mind. Five might as well have been a hundred. With care, that much money could feed us for a month. We could not afford five dollars worth of buttons for a dress that would most likely never be worn, not even to keep a dream alive. I refused to say it out loud, however.

41

Even if my mind was failing, as long as I had free choice, I would still believe in our plan.

"Well, when we get the dress made, we'll see what buttons we can manage."

Our conversation faded into the creak of the wagon and Jeremiah's plodding footsteps. We were nearing our own drive when I saw another wagon approaching in the distance. My heart picked up its beat and my hands tightened on the reins. If more soldiers were on the road I thought I might run screaming into the woods and stay there. I couldn't leave my sisters, however. I pushed the sack with Papa's pistol toward Victoria, and understanding, she bent and lifted it to her lap.

We met the wagon at the very end of our own drive. Long before that, I had calmed down because this wagon was obviously real, if unusual. It was a tinker's wagon, the kind that used to follow the army selling necessities and trinkets. As it pulled up facing us, the dapper, cleanly dressed driver doffed his hat and bowed from his perch on the wagon seat.

"Ladies," he said.

I nodded. "Mr.?"

"Tucker," he answered with a smile. "As in the song, 'Ol' Dan Tucker, he rode to town,'" he sang.

The man had to be at least our father's age the year he'd left us and was obviously a charmer. He didn't seem to have been soured by the end of the war as so many of those who'd made their living off of it had. But then again, he wasn't a southerner, that much was clear from his accent.

"Nice to meet you, sir," I said. "This is the end of our drive, we're from the Oak Creek plantation." I did my best to make it sound grander than it was. A northerner who wandered the roads might take family land for granted. I did not.

"I was wondering how far it is to the nearest town?" he asked.

"Stoneman is a bit over two miles." I indicated the road we'd just driven.

"Well, thank you. I have less of a journey than I thought. Is there anything you ladies would like to look at on my wagon?" He winked at Claire. "I have some wonderous things. Some of them all the way from London, England."

Victoria spoke up, saving me from being the spoilsport. "Thank you, but no, sir." She slid her hand off the sack with the pistol in her lap and grasped Claire's hand, in comfort, I suppose. "We wouldn't want to waste your time. As you can see we've just come from town and purchased our supplies. We have no extra coin left for trinkets."

Tinker Tucker scratched his head before putting his hat back on. He looked at Claire once more, then faced me. "I'll trade you some of my time if you'll allow me to water my horse. My stalwart companion here hasn't had a drop since morning."

I looked at Victoria. How could we refuse? None of us would deny an animal water. Victoria nodded then placed her hand back on the pistol.

"Of course, you must follow us," she said to the tinker. "Water is the one thing in plentiful supply at Oak Creek."

Half an hour later, I pulled back the lace sheers and watched from the window as Claire, with Victoria not too far away, ooohed and aaaahed over the tinker's wares. Occasionally Claire would take something over to show Victoria, and they would both smile or hold the item up to the light. I smiled too, enjoying the show. The tinker talked and talked and managed to coax quite a bit of conversation out of shy Claire and suspicious Victoria. For a moment the present seemed more like the past, before our tragedies, when a tinker could brighten any day with a clever poem or a hair riband.

After the tinker's horse had drunk his fill and rested, Mr. Tucker began to repack his wagon in preparation to leave, and the spell was broken. Before he closed up the last cupboard I saw him hand Claire something. Claire shook her head no and tried to give the item back. The man tipped his hat and put his hands in his pockets.

My ire rose. Was he still determined to sell my little sister something? I descended on the group as an avenging angel might fly into battle.

"Julia, tell Mr. Tucker I can't take these," Claire begged. There were tears in her eyes and I hardened my heart before I turned to the man.

He held up a large calloused hand. "Now I know you can't pay, and I don't want you to. The young lady said she's getting married, and I'm feeling homesick for my own family in Illinois. Please allow me to contribute a gift for your family."

Some of my anger faded. If he truly wanted to give Claire a trinket, then I suppose it would be all right, although I wouldn't allow him to think us beggars. I turned to Claire. "Let me see what this controversy is about."

Claire swallowed, and as she raised her hand, I could see that it was shaking. I looked at what she held and felt as though lightning had struck nearby and caused my hair to stand on end.

Twenty-four pearl buttons, neatly sewn on to a card. The exact buttons Claire had pined for at Mr. Tate's. I felt the sudden need to sit down and immediately did so on the front steps. Victoria rushed to my side and even Tinker Tucker had a worried look on his face. I kept staring at Claire. She seemed as flummoxed as I.

"Are you all right, miss?" Mr. Tucker asked.

I drew in a deep breath and looked up at him. "Sir, if you feel you can afford to give my sister such a gift, then yes, I'm all right. Let us say I am stunned by your generosity."

He reached down to help me stand again. "It's just as well she has them," he said with a modest shrug. "I don't have much call for fine things such as they. Especially weddin' things in these times. The war is over and I'm headin' south to Carolina. Gonna sell the whole kit and caboodle before I light out for home. A card of buttons won't make or break the sale." He nodded to Claire. "Have them with my good wishes, miss."

He tried to leave then, but we wouldn't

hear of it. He declined dinner, saying he wanted to get farther along before dark. We convinced him that at the very least we could pack him a basket of cold food for his ride.

By that evening, long after the tinker's wagon rolled off down our drive, I knew I could wait no longer before discussing the day with Victoria.

"I need to speak with you," I said as Victoria put away her handwork in preparation for going upstairs to bed. She nodded and sat back down facing me.

Without preamble, I recited the events of the afternoon on Thomasville Road. I faltered a few times when what I had to say seemed utterly outlandish even to me, but I persisted with every detail I could remember.

Victoria's initial reaction was not what I had expected. After describing the spirit faces of soldiers long dead, my sister looked on me with intense longing in her eyes. "I wish I had seen them," she said softly.

Struck dumb for the third time that day, I reminded myself to continue breathing. Then I found my voice. "What are you saying? Do you realize I may be delirious or demented? You may have to lock me in the root cellar if this goes on."

Victoria was shaking her head no before I even finished speaking. "You are not demented and I will never lock you in a cellar," she said with amusement playing around her mouth. "Something more than your sanity, or lack of it, is at work here. There are too many other odd things happening."

I took another deep breath and calmly folded my flapping hands into my lap. Having my sister take the wind out of my terror did much to calm me. "What do you mean?"

"I believe that somehow we are getting what we'd wished and prayed for. We set out to give Claire a wedding dress and a wedding. Since then, we've been gifted in one way or another with all the pieces needed for her dress, first lace and thread, then buttons."

I started to interrupt, but Victoria stopped me.

"I have no idea what long-dead soldiers have to do with our quest, but as you said, we must have some backbone about this. As long as a ghost doesn't knock on our door, and as long as things appear to work toward our purpose, we should be grateful and keep believing." She looked away for a moment, toward the window. "I truly wish

I had seen them, though."

"So you don't think I'm a lunatic?" I asked, halfway teasing.

She smiled as she gazed at me again. "If you are, then you have been so all your life and that's the way we want you." I laughed as she stood. "The next time you see them, sound the alarm," she said. "I want to get a good look." After patting my shoulder, she took herself upstairs.

Chapter Four

Two weeks went by without incident. We worked on the dress a bit each day with deliberation. When it was time to claim our smoked meat from the Pelton farm, Victoria rode along with me, just in case I again met up with any spirits on the road. We saw none and even more telling, Jeremiah was as pluggish as ever. The only odd occurrence happened at the farm itself.

The Peltons were known for three things in this area. They were masters at hunting, butchering and smoking meat, and for being pecuniary. They wasted nothing and gave away little without a price. The other side of that equation spoke to the fact that they also wouldn't cheat you, since cheating *them* would be dangerous. We'd often joked that "an eye for an eye" must be carved on the family crest.

They'd lost two sons to the war. One to typhus and the other to the guns of the Federals at Chancellorsville.

As Victoria and I watched the younger Pelton sons load our winter's worth of ham, bacon, sausage, and fatback into the wagon, Mr. Pelton came out to oversee. Victoria and I managed to keep up a stunted conversation with the man even though his clothes were covered with old blood and soot smears. When he mentioned they'd had a good crop of pumpkins for the year, we decided to look over the excess for sale.

We were placing the two pumpkins we'd bought for a penny in the back of the wagon when I casually studied the wrapped packages of meat. There seemed to be one large package too many. Better safe than in disgrace, I brought the matter up with one of the younger Peltons.

"I believe you've given us one package too many," I said and pointed to the two large bundles wrapped in sacking.

The boy, who was big for his age but could barely be in his teen years, tugged at his sleeve and answered, "No, mum."

I went to the side of the wagon and tapped the package closest to me. "These two, right here," I said.

He merely shook his head no and walked away. A moment later he came back with his father who now had fresh blood on the leather apron around his middle.

"Mr. Pelton," I began. "I believe you've given us too much meat. Have you forgotten your portion for the work?"

"It's all there," Mr. Pelton said.

Thinking I had insulted him, I quickly said, "Of course, I know it's all there, sir. As a matter of fact, it seems to be more than we brought you."

"It's all there," he said again, and I was beginning to think I had wandered off the track again. I looked at Victoria and she shrugged her shoulders. Mr. Pelton seemed eager to get back to work, yet in the following moment, he finally shed some light on our disagreement. "In the spring, before the weddin' I'll send one of my boys over with some venison," he said. Then, with the raise of a bloody hand, and before we could speak our gratitude, he turned and walked away followed by his son.

"Now if that doesn't frost the cake," I said as we drove away. "Anders Pelton giving something away. I believe we've just witnessed a miracle."

Instead of the smile I'd expected, Victoria looked as serious as a Sunday school teacher explaining judgment day. "It seems as though this entire county is in on our marriage plan. And that, no doubt, is a wonderful thing. Soon we'll have every-thing we need save the groom."

The groom.

That would be the problem, I thought. How to find a suitable husband in the slim numbers after the war? Not to mention a man who would love and cherish our sister.

"If there is no wedding in the spring, we'll have to give back what we can and pay for the rest. It wouldn't be right, other-wise," I admitted.

"Julia Lovejoy," Victoria admonished, calling me by the name I'd barely gotten used to before my husband expired. "Of course there will be a wedding in the spring. These gifts only go to prove our faith." She eyed me severely. "Now gather your faith and hush. We have much to do."

During the first week of December we attached the embroidered bodice to the twelve-paneled skirt of Claire's dress. There was still quite a bit of handwork to be done but we'd progressed to a point where we could have a fitting. On the eve-ning of December sixth, we built a roaring fire in our parlor fireplace, lit all the lamps, and soon had Claire standing in the center of the braided rug, shivering in her stocking feet, corset, chemise, and petticoats.

As we prepared to help Claire into the gown, by silent consensus, we stopped for a moment. I looked at Victoria and she took Claire's hand. The occasion somehow seemed momentous because of our work, but more so because of all the unbidden help we'd received. At Victoria's urging, we again pledged our faith in the enterprise as we had on that last night of October. A very few moments later, solemnly, as if we were anointing her with vestments, we slipped the dress over Claire's head and settled it on her hips and shoulders.

She looked lovely. The dress fit perfectly, and as I stared at my "little" sister, the glow on her face seemed to transform her. She kept turning this way and that, trying to get a true glimpse of her gown. In unfettered excitement, Victoria and I hurried to what had been our mother's room and hauled out the framed cheval mirror which had been one of her prize possessions. We set it in front of Claire so that she might get a good view.

The effect was unexpected. Instead of a beatific smile from the soon-to-be bride, Claire reverently touched the lace at her bosom, and burst into tears.

Victoria and I stood the mirror against the wall and moved to her side. I put my arm about her waist and pulled her head to my shoulder. "What is this now, Clarey?" I asked, perplexed. I hoped she'd say she was overcome with joy but I didn't truly feel that to be the case.

"It's so — so beaut— so beautiful," she hiccoughed between her tears. "You've bo— both done so mu— much for me."

I pushed her mussed hair back and waited for the seed of her tears.

"You know I'll never be a bride," she added, her voice muffled and low, directed more to the collar of my dress than to Victoria and me.

Well, on the positive side, it was good to know that Claire at least had retained her sanity. If she had blindly believed this dress-without-a-groom plan, then I would have thought her too fragile for the constant vagaries of fate. She was demonstrating that her feet were firmly planted on the family ground of Oak Creek Plantation, no matter how high her dreams had flown her heart.

Victoria put her arms around the two of us. "Come, come now," she said. "You cannot know the future. None of us can." She squeezed us tight. "And you at least are ahead of the game. When the right man comes along, you'll have a gown worthy of your love. There'll be none of this, 'What shall I wear?' "

It sounded good, I thought. I waited, feeling Claire's defeated weight against my shoulder. Her hiccoughing had ceased, but I couldn't see to measure her tears.

Finally, she raised her head. "I suppose you're right. As long as I don't get as fat as Mrs. Pembroke, the Reverend's wife, I can wear it into my old age." She tried to smile then, but it wavered at the edges. She was being brave for us rather than counting her blessings. Dear girl.

"That's right," Victoria agreed, then stepped away and faced us in a business-like manner. "But I don't believe you'll have to wait that long. Now, let's see how much more we have to do yet."

The storm had passed, but a bit of the excitement had traveled with it. A shame, I thought as I helped Victoria mark the hemline. A verifiable shame if we couldn't make this real. Victoria's frown came back to me from past times when I had wandered off the path of the faithful. My sister, I decided, was becoming a zealot about this wedding business. Well, it wasn't spring yet, not even Christmas. We had time to work any magic we could muster.

The letter came a week later.

We hadn't had mail in months, and much toward the end had been bad news. So long had passed that when the letter arrived, brought by a young boy on a mule, Victoria and I simply looked at each other. One wanting the other to accept the well-traveled envelope. Claire took matters into her hands and snatched the letter as if it was a fish and might get away.

"It's for you Julia," she said and held the missive out to me. For one wild moment I relived the heart-pounding times I'd received treasured letters from William. Because of the war they had been few and far between. Now instead of excitement, I felt only dread. But I forced myself to act. My hand accepted the letter and my fingers rubbed over my own name, written on the front. I did not recognize the script. Without pausing for further deliberation or sadness, I opened the envelope.

Dear Mrs. Lovejoy,

I hope this letter finds you in good health and spirit. I realize this introduction is somewhat improper, but I fear that many improprieties have taken the place of civilized manners after the war.

Allow me to introduce myself. I am Sgt. Monroe Tacy, late of the CSA. I had the

honor of serving with your husband Lieu-
tenant Lovejoy. I was given the unhappy
duty of writing to you after his death.

I remembered the name. How could I
not? It had been bitter and hard to lose my
William, but at least this man, this fellow
soldier had sent me what little comfort
there was to send.

I hope you have fared well in these last
two years. If goodwill has served you in
your grief, then I must admit that part of it
came from me. Lieutenant Lovejoy was a
fine soldier, a gentleman, and my friend.
Because of that, I do have more news for
you on his behalf. When I wrote to you, our
unit was doing its utmost to recover from
our losses on Cemetery Ridge at Gettys-
burg, so I could not tell you all. I had no
notion as to whether I would live long
enough to complete William's request. Now
that I have by some miracle been returned
whole and alive to my family, I have one
more mission on Lieutenant Lovejoy's be-
half to perform.

Would you permit me to visit you and
your family after the New Year? When
you see what I bring with me, you will
understand the importance of my per-

sonal attention to its delivery. If this is satisfactory, please post a missive with your instructions. I shall follow them to the letter.

At your service,
Monroe Tacy, Savannah 1865

I sat looking at the letter for a very long time. Both Claire and Victoria had wandered off to other chores, leaving me alone, knowing I would inform them of the contents when I was ready.

By William's request.

What was I to think? Yes, of course I wanted any token of William that remained on this Earth. But this letter, this friend of William's who would do his bidding, would only bring back the past, would make me long for things that could not be. I had no stamina to live through old pain.

There was enough new pain to take its place.

Our survival, that of my sisters and of our family, had overridden my grief. I had no time to wail at how the past might have been different or how another outcome for William would have changed my life. Sergeant Tacy could not help in this, he could only trip me up on my forward path. Could I bear to look into the eyes of the man who had watched my beloved draw his last breath?

Claire and Victoria had other ideas of course. When I read the letter to them, they had distinctly different reactions. Claire, who had barely known William but had witnessed my happiness, was emphatic and quite dramatic about allowing his last request to be fulfilled.

"Can you imagine how much he loved you, Julia? That on his dying breath he sent a token to his wife?"

Of course I'd shed tears over that idea two years before when I'd received the first letter from the Sergeant. What Claire didn't understand was that no matter how much one loved, maintaining or falling into an unfathomable depth of grief ultimately killed the soul. I had come very close to that point before recognizing it. Grief could, if left unfettered, become the purpose of a life rather than a tribute to lost love. I was determined not to be tempted into it again.

"Why do you suppose he has waited so long to make this visit?" Victoria asked, ever vigilant for knots in the logic of things.

"Perhaps it takes longer for living soldiers to conclude their warring business than those who died. A cipher in a ledger is orderly and without cause or promises to keep," I said, because I had no idea.

"What will you do?" Claire asked as she handed the letter back.

I looked at them both and could feel their concern. I wanted to give Claire an answer, but if one existed inside me, I did not know it. "I will have to think on this awhile," I said.

Victoria nodded and rose to her feet. After patting her skirts into place she touched Claire's shoulder. "Come help me start supper," she said. I put the letter aside and started to rise. Victoria shook her head. "We can manage on our own," she assured me.

Without the will to argue, I let them go. After a few moments, I stood and moved closer to the sitting room windows that looked out on the side yard, to what used to be our mother's rose garden. We'd had no time for it in two years. Out of necessity, our efforts were required in the kitchen garden to greens and beans. We couldn't eat roses. The garden space remained, but many of the old rose bushes had fallen into weedy disarray, as if they knew that my mother, Amelia, was no longer here to walk among them and admire the scents.

The weather had turned colder and the air smelled like snow. Fall had become winter. Soon the roses would be blanketed until spring. I felt like my heart had been blanketed as well. Cold protection from an even colder fate. The letter called to me one more time and I brought it up to the light. *What am I to do, William? Did you intend to keep your memory alive so that I would forever feel the pain of your loss? Or did you simply wish to exhibit your love?*

Tears blurred my vision. I resolutely folded the page and returned it to the envelope. I decided to wait, at least for the night, to make a decision. If the dream came to me again, I would refuse Sergeant Tacy's offer. If it did not, I would have to make the decision on my own.

It snowed during the night. I woke up to a bright dawn with the world in utter silence, the muffled quiet only a snowfall can produce. Instead of leaving the warmth provided by the quilts on my bed, I remained as still as the world outside, thinking. The dream had not returned. I was grateful for that blessing. I'd even placed Sergeant Tacy's letter under my pillow to tempt fate. There were enough unconnected thoughts running through my head for me to relish adding another round of grief to the mix. But the letter had remained harmless, bringing neither sadness nor enlightenment. It was up to me to make the decision, and I swore before leaving my bed to make one by sunset.

The snow crunched and squeaked under our feet as Victoria and I walked down the drive. The world had been transformed, becoming a place of black and white like a pen and ink sketch. I had wanted to get outside and Victoria asked if she could walk with me. Now we were bundled up in gloves and shawls on this bright, still day, making tracks in the fresh snow.

I didn't waste any time choosing the subject. "What do you think about this letter business?" I asked.

Victoria took several more steps before answering. Finally, she said, "I think it's interesting that it came from Savannah."

That stopped me and I turned to her in surprise. "Savannah?"

"Yes," she went on. "The one other city where we have family, however distant."

"How does that apply to this letter?"

"At the very least we could obtain some

information about the Sergeant, if you are concerned about his interest in a widow several states away." She glanced toward the road at the end of the drive. "At the most, we could have him deliver William's token to our cousin for safekeeping, and you may collect it at your will."

Of a sudden, every thread of my being revolted. "No," I said. "If the man is willing to bring whatever William sent from the dead, then I want it in my hands. No other's."

Victoria smiled, and as simply as that, I realized I'd made the decision. She took my arm and started me moving again toward the road. "I thought as much."

We walked in silence the rest of the way, our skirts growing heavier with the weight of wet snow. When we reached the board fence, the boundary of our world, we both brushed away the snow and leaned on the rail, gazing at the white landscape around us. There were no signs of human movement except for our own footprints and swirls from our skirts marking the pristine white. I pointed down the road a ways at the prints made by a rabbit, knowing that if we walked another several yards we'd surely see deer tracks.

Victoria picked up the thread of our conversation. "I would like to have had some word from James."

I immediately felt lower than a viper for dillydallying over a letter that could be viewed as an embarrassment of riches when Victoria had had nothing. We'd never spoken at length about her feelings for her husband. In simpler times it just wasn't done, and when times grew hard, there wasn't opportunity or luxury. Now, however, my sister and I had all the time in the world.

"Did you love him?" I asked.

She seemed to think it over. "He was a very sweet, scholarly man," she said finally, not truly answering the question. "I despaired of him surviving the harshness of a war." She gazed at me. "And as we both know, he did not." She dropped her gaze then. "But yes, in answer to your question, I did love him. Ours was a quiet, content kind of love. We were well suited."

I angled my arm around her and squeezed her shoulders. "I'm sorry he didn't come back to you, Vee. As sorry as I am about my William."

She smiled sadly toward the empty road. "Thank you, Jules. Do you think we'll see them again someday?" she asked, sounding younger and unsure.

"I don't doubt it," I said fiercely. "If God in heaven decided he needed our men more than we did, then at least he can see fit to give them back when we pass over." I was looking at Victoria's profile as I spoke. Suddenly, she gasped in a little breath and opened her mouth. No sound came out, however. She lifted a gloved hand and pointed.

As I looked, I felt each hair at the back of my neck prickle from the swift rush of coldness racing down my spine. In the distance, a hundred yards or so down the road, I saw men walking . . . no, marching. There were no horses this time, but the colors were there. The Stars and Bars of the disbanded Confederacy and the blue flag of Virginia.

My knees wobbled, and Victoria put an arm about my waist to support me. The look on her face gave me another chill. There was no fear there, no shock. Her eyes blazed with interest and pride.

The men came closer, and the same phenomenon occurred as I had witnessed before. There was no sound. Not even wind in the trees or boots on snow. The grayness remained as well, although these men were in higher spirits and better physical shape than the group I'd seen on Thomasville Road.

The white of the snow and sky was dazzling. Victoria and I remained like living statues at the fence rail, as if we were the sole guests at a patriotic parade. For a moment I wondered if those who lost sons and husbands in the north had witnessed anything like this. But then the men were nearly upon us, and I couldn't think at all, I could only watch.

Their eyes were trained on some distant point. Some of their uniforms were pieced and patched, others mismatched. But these men still had some fight left in them, you could see it. The eerie transparency swam along their shoulders and boots, as if they walked through water but there was no sound, no smell, no —

Halfway past, one of them on our side pulled his gaze away from the horizon and looked directly at my sister and me. Victoria's grip on my waist grew painful but I saw her smile. The soldier smiled back and tipped his dusty cap.

Then, they were gone.

I heard my name being called from a distance. It was Claire, no, Victoria. I couldn't tell. I felt cold and hot at the same time. When I opened my eyes, both my sisters were staring down at me. Claire looked terrified. I would learn later that she'd run all the way from the house when she'd seen me fall. But Victoria . . . Victoria looked as fey as I'd ever seen her. She actually laughed as she made Claire take my hand and pull me up from where I'd landed in the snow.

"Are you all right?" Victoria asked, but I could tell she knew that I was.

"I think I —" I glanced toward the road again. "I just had a slight dizzy spell," I assured them, or rather Claire. Victoria knew exactly what had happened, and I felt so foolish I didn't want to offer the truth to be reexamined. "You got your wish," was all I said to her.

"I did indeed," she said, grinning. "Thank you."

I was momentarily mesmerized by her unbridled joy. Then I realized she thought I had somehow produced the show we'd just witnessed. "Me? Believe me, I don't know what makes it happen. . . ."

"What are you two talking about?" Claire demanded, a little surly after being frightened.

Victoria took Claire by the arm and started back toward the house. "You see, Jules and I had a little bet that she couldn't hold her breath for long in this cold air, so —" She stopped and waited. "Can you make it back on your own?" she asked me.

Still a bit dazed by the vision and her reaction, I nodded, letting them go. I needed
to think, about the strangeness in the air,
the uncanny sight we'd just witnessed.
Somewhere among my wonderment, I
found the sparkling recognition that I
could not be losing my sanity after all. Not
unless the entire family was in the same
position. Victoria had seen them, too. And
beyond that, one of them had seen her.

I turned and studied the road one more
time, trying to fathom the meaning. Not a
footprint or dent marred the fresh snow. A
small portion of Victoria's elation touched
me. For whatever reason, we could see soldiers who'd been dead for a year or more.
They were belatedly making their way
home. A shudder went through me, and I
fervently prayed that my William and Vee's
James could find their way as well.

At that moment I realized that I stood
alone at the fence while my sisters were
halfway to the house. Not wishing to press
fate, I hurried to catch up with them.

Chapter Five

I wrote to Sergeant Tacy that evening.

Dear Sir:
Your letter finds me in a state of surprise. Not because of any impropriety, but rather concerning the space of time between this letter and the last. I remember your name well and wish you to know that your news from the battlefield greatly eased my mind on the matter of my husband's death.
As to my health and spirit, I am faring as well as any in these times. And again, I thank you for your kind thoughts. I cannot imagine what you hold that would have you make such a long trip to visit us in Virginia. But, if you wish to do so, my sisters and I offer what hospitality we can gather. The accommodations are meager, I'm afraid. We only have a parson's room or the barn for sleeping.
Christmas is nearly upon us. If you will advise me the anticipated time of your ar-

rival, we will do our best to make a fine welcome.

> *I remain,*
> *Mrs. Julia Lovejoy*

Christmas came and went. We spent the morning decorating the house with spruce and holly, paying special attention to the portraits of our much beloved and sorely missed parents. We attended services and had our miracle ham for dinner. We also, with some ceremony, each took a turn at sewing the pearl buttons on Claire's gown. It was nearly finished, only the hemming and fitting remained. The time to shift our campaign from dressmaking to out-and-out husband hunting had come. The discussion that evening was heated.

"It's unseemly to inquire about the marital status of every man we meet," Victoria reminded us in a voice so much like our mother's I had to smile.

She was referring to my own transgression after services when I boldly asked Mrs. Donahoe about her cousin just in from Ireland. The question tripped up the grand dame momentarily, but then she gazed at me with some pity in her eyes, no doubt thinking that my widowhood had lost its charm, and informed me her cousin had arrived in anticipation of bringing his enceinte wife and two other children at such time as was financially feasible. Then she changed the subject to Claire's upcoming wedding, and I had to retreat as soon as decently possible before I ran completely out of lies.

"Thank you *Lady* Victoria for that sterling advice," I said, mimicking Mrs. Habersham, a deportment teacher we'd been forced to suffer instruction from years earlier. The irony as we now knew it was that she'd taught us skills we had no use for other than fine needlework. At this point no one cared if we walked like ladies, could recite poetry, or properly serve tea to the queen. But the world was different then.

A smile curved Victoria's lips. "You're welcome, Lady Julia. And have you learned your lesson?"

"Most assuredly," I answered. Claire remained excluded since she had not experienced the wooden ruler Mrs. Habersham could wield with deadly accuracy.

A few moments of silence filled only with the ticking of the clock on the sideboard left us to our own thoughts. Then Victoria, in her own calm and deliberate manner, dropped a lightning bolt in the center of the room.

"I've been thinking," she said. "When we hear back from your Sergeant Tacy, as I have no doubt we will, and set a date for his visit . . ." She drew the moment out until I could have screamed.

"Yes?" I prompted.

Victoria raised her eyes and stared directly into mine. "I think we should ask him to accompany you and Claire south, back to our cousin in Savannah. After we ascertain his good character, of course," she added quickly. "He has to return there in any case. . . ."

I was surprised into silence. But Claire's vocal abilities made up for us both. "Oh Julia! Could we? Go to Savannah, I mean?" She dashed from her chair and took a seat at my feet so she could plead more effectively.

"But that would leave you here alone," I said to Victoria, the only part of her plan which registered in my spinning mind.

"You're not afraid, are you Victoria?" Claire looked up at me. "We could go for a little while and be back before Vee got lonely."

"Whoa!" I said, trying to slow down this runaway idea. "What if Sergeant Tacy isn't returning directly to Savannah? Suppose he doesn't want the responsibility of two unmarried women on his hands?" I directed the next question at Victoria. "Suppose our cousins have forgotten our existence, or worse, don't want to reestablish our meager connection?"

"On that point, I have taken the liberty of writing them a letter."

"You what?" Totally befuddled by what felt like a mutiny, I stared at my sister. This was so unlike her, to take the bit in her teeth without proper discussion and agreement, that I wondered briefly if seeing the soldiers on the road had done something to *her* mind. Then I almost laughed. Me, accusing Victoria of acting rashly. Talk about the kettle calling the pot black.

Claire changed her loyalty then and there. She moved from the rug at my feet to the chair adjacent to Victoria — her new champion.

"Traitor," I said. Claire grinned at me, unrepentant. "Is there more to this plan?" I asked Victoria. "Such as where we might acquire the coin to pay for such a trip?" I heard my own words sounding mulish and sighed. "Never mind," I said. "If our cousins will have us, we shall plot a way to get there."

Claire jumped to her feet and made a waltzing circuit of the room. If nothing else, we had made her a happy Christmas. Later, when Victoria and I were alone, the real plotting began. I was beginning to believe my sister much more talented at faith in miracles than I. So, I had to ask . . .

"Do you think we'll have an easier time finding Claire a husband in Savannah? We *are* in poor circumstances."

"As is the rest of the South," she pronounced as she turned down the lamp. "I think at this point all we need do is concentrate on ways to charm your Sergeant into getting the two of you there. I will charm our cousin into accepting you. A trip to Savannah itself will do much to mitigate the grief of having our husband-out-of-air scheme come to nothing."

"In other words, we will be giving Claire one thing she wished for."

"Exactly," she said. "By the time the Sergeant arrives we should have a scheme in place. Perhaps you could beg the favor as the widow of his good friend, William."

I bridled at that, and since I was in the process of turning down the other lamp, Vee could see my face clearly.

"Think for a moment, Julia. I know your pride is such that you'd never play on William's death. You never asked his family for a thing. But this is different. This is" —

she searched for the words — "war. A different kind of war — one that must be fought after the losses of the other. Keep in mind we do this for Claire, for our family. Our motives are pure. Anything we have to do, short of completely ruining ourselves, should be permitted, embraced even. Only God may judge us."

The same God who took William and James from us. I was appalled by my blasphemous thoughts and decided it was time to end the discussion. Oh, I would agree to help, to plot, and to play my part. But I had not decided how to do that yet. We had time, we hadn't received a return post from the Sergeant. As soon as we did, the campaign would commence.

In bed that night, I abandoned puny worries about my grief and its reappearance in my life and began counting money. Well, not money precisely, but assets. We had a hatbox full of Confederate script which would burn easier than it would spend. My father had left us the beneficiaries to a few investments, half of which had fallen with the South. But Papa's interest in an English textile company had survived, though it was not of huge consequence. We'd paid our taxes with the proceeds and bartering had kept us in food and lamp oil. But time was coming when we'd need help. We couldn't survive by living in the house while the fields stayed fallow and the barn fell into disrepair.

Spending any money on a visit to Savannah seemed more than folly. It seemed like lunacy.

And yet, I had to find a way.

As I twisted my hands together in thought, I felt the familiar pressure of my wedding ring. My *gold* wedding ring. I hadn't taken it from my finger since William had placed it there. Could I part with it? He had worn his unto death. Were my words of getting past my grief only delusions? Experimentally, I twisted the ring off my finger. The world did not shatter or come to an end. No thunderclaps or lightning strikes, no catastrophe of any kind except for the vacancy feeling unfamiliar. I rested in the dark, seeing in my mind Claire's stricken face at the prospect of never having an opportunity, and hearing my own words coming back to haunt me. I'd told Victoria, "You and I have had our opportunities."

In these slim times, gold was gold. Holding on to my ring would not bring William back to me. And if giving it up meant one more step on the crazy road we trod, then I could not withhold it. Keeping that thought firmly in mind, I dozed off with the ring clutched in my hand, already having said good-bye.

"What have you done with your ring?" Victoria asked nearly a week later. The three of us were in the cookhouse making supper. An activity which prevented me from hiding my hands.

I had worn the ring until the opportunity arose to visit town on my own and sell it to Mr. Tate for a few dollars, hoping against hope its disappearance would be overlooked. I should have known better.

"I've lost it," I said.

"Oh, no," Claire said, believing me. "When did you last see it? You should have told us and we could have helped search."

Victoria merely continued to stare at me. It was unnerving the way she seemed to be able to sort through my thoughts. In agitation I left the task of scraping salsify roots and moved over to check the heat of the stove. That way I wouldn't have to look either of them in the eye.

"I didn't notice it missing until I dressed for bed. I might have dropped it anywhere."

"We'll need to keep an eye out, won't

we, Claire?" Victoria said.

"Yes," Claire responded, then less enthusiastically added, "I'm sorry you lost it, Julia. I know it meant the world to you."

The world. This farm and my two sisters were all the world I cared about now. I would sell more than my ring to keep them happy and safe. Claire had unintentionally made me feel better about the entire enterprise even though she'd been unaware. "Thank you, sister," I answered.

Within an hour, Victoria had me cornered once again.

"When I said we should find a way to get Claire to Savannah, I didn't mean for you to sell everything you own," she fumed.

"I didn't sell everything. I sold something that only claimed sentimental value. Whether I wear that ring or not, I will always be William's wife."

Victoria relented with a sigh. "I know," she said, slipping an arm around my waist. "But why didn't you talk to me? We might have thought of something else." She brought her own hand up and gazed at the ring on her finger. The one James had given her. "I would say we would sell mine as well, but it's only tin and wouldn't bring but a few pennies."

"I didn't get as much for mine as I'd

hoped. We may have to sell something else. But I want to wait and see what we hear from Sergeant Tacy before we strip the house bare. He may not even agree to the scheme." I gave Victoria a squeeze and walked toward the dining room. "We still have to make it through this winter as well."

"Spring will be upon us before we know it," Victoria said with conviction.

"No doubt," I replied. "And I'm sure Claire will keep us apprised of each day passing between now and then."

Chapter Six

After keeping us company through Christmas and New Year's Day, the snow deserted us the first week in January. The world outside went back to its usual selection of browns, blacks, and grays. Except for the sky. The sky remained a brilliant, robin's egg blue with only a few puffy clouds overhead. It was on one of those bright, clear days, January sixth, that another letter from Sergeant Tacy arrived.

Madam,

I am extremely happy to hear that you are well and in good circumstances, and I'm very grateful for the hospitality you offer. I assure you, after marching for two years and sleeping on cold, hard ground most of those nights, any barn or closet that contains a mattress of hay will seem a palace to me.

I am sending this letter to alert you to my arrival. I plan to leave Savannah by train on the fifteenth. Barring any further disruption by construction on the tracks, I should be in your area no later than the twenty-fifth of January. If, for any reason, this is unsatisfactory, please inform me on return post.

Your servant,
Monroe Tacy

"Three weeks," I said, feeling as though I'd been dropped onto the back of a wild horse and could not let go for fear of falling. I gazed up at Victoria. "He'll be here in three weeks."

"Then we'll be able to leave for Savannah?" Claire asked, clasping her hands together in an effort to remain dignified in her excitement.

"Not right away," Victoria answered. "We must persuade him to take you two first. I've given this some thought. I believe the best way to convince him that you and Julia would be suitable traveling companions is to show him you are confident, self-managing, and above all, well behaved."

Claire looked to me to interpret. "What she means is we have to show Sergeant Tacy we wouldn't be any trouble to him, that we know how to mind our manners."

"Of course, we'd be no trouble . . ." Claire began.

"In these times, we have no idea what type of trouble might await travelers. That is something he'll likely see fit to enlighten us about. We must prepare some answers to his obvious questions, such as. Do we have our own funds? Do we expect him to provide anything beyond his escort? But Vee is right, we also need to be on our best behavior and exhibit all our charm."

Victoria continued her planning. "We'll make a list, first to get this house in order, then to ready the barn or parson's room for his use. I think it would be wise to bring out some extra food for his welcome. Julia, do we have enough makings and sugar for a vinegar pie?"

"I believe so."

"Claire, you must choose three of your newer dresses and begin freshening them the best you can. If you need help with darning or hemming, I'll volunteer." Victoria turned to me. "Julia, you'll need to do the same. . . ."

And so it began. We prepared for Sergeant Tacy's arrival no less carefully than Robert E. Lee had ever planned the movements of his army. Of course, we hoped to be more successful in the outcome. By the twenty-fifth winter had revisited, decorating Oak Creek in alabaster while we'd scrubbed and scraped, boiled and baked. We'd even swept the newly accumulated snow off the front steps.

Then, we waited.

Claire spent most of her time at the window while Victoria and I displayed ourselves in our second and third best dresses respectively, filling our time with needlework or reading. After waiting through dinner, Claire could not remain still any longer. She put on a heavy shawl and went outside to walk in the snow and breathe new air. No doubt to will the man closer by meeting him partway.

I hadn't lost my patience yet, but I knew all our nerves were worn thin. We'd worked as hard in the last few weeks as we'd ever worked, and now the inactivity felt unfamiliar and somehow foreboding. Heaven forbid should we receive a message saying the good Sergeant had changed his mind. I had reread the same line in the book I held three times when I heard Claire's scream. I dropped the book to the floor.

Both Victoria and I reached the front door at the same instant. I yanked it open and she charged outside first. From the porch we could see Claire running full tilt through the fallow cornfield toward the house. She'd lost her shawl and she had her skirts rucked up to run like a hoyden through the snow.

"Go to her. I'll get the pistol." I couldn't imagine what had frightened her so, but whatever it was, I'd be glad to put a hole in it.

By the time I retrieved the pistol and followed Victoria outside, I found both my sisters collapsed in the snow, their skirts like two colorful water lilies on a pond of white. Claire was still shaking and blubbering while Victoria held her with a herculean embrace.

"What's happened?" I asked, grasping the grip of the pistol in my cold fingers and looking toward the other side of the cornfield. If someone was chasing my sister, then I wanted enough time to aim with my shaking hands.

"Claire believes she's seen a ghost," Victoria said.

That took the air out of me. I looked down at Victoria but didn't know what to say.

"I *did* see a ghost," Claire insisted.

My nerves had been frayed to the point of dilapidation. Heedless of my third-best dress, I sat down in the snow next to Claire and released my death grip on the pistol. "Tell me what you saw," I asked.

Claire sniffed and straightened out of Victoria's arms. She held on to her hand, however.

"Well, I was walking out toward the road — Powder Mill Road." She turned and pointed in the direction we knew she'd gone since she'd come back directly. Her footprints remained visible in the snow. "I thought to see if I could spy our visitor in the distance. But I didn't see him." She faltered and looked down at her hand clasped with Victoria's.

Victoria hugged her briefly. "Tell us, Clarey. We'll believe you."

"I sa— saw a ghost," Claire stuttered out.

"One ghost?" I asked, thinking she'd surely seen the same thing Victoria and I had seen on the road. Soldiers.

"Yes, only one." She pressed her free hand to her chest. "If I'd seen more, I'd have died of fright surely."

Perhaps this spirit had nothing to do with our other ghosts. By this rate we might find ourselves changing the name of the plantation to Oak Creek Cemetery and residing among the dearly departed rather than living neighbors. There seemed to be more ghosts than people in this corner of the county.

"What did he look like?" I asked. Then, could have bit my tongue.

"How did you know it was a he?" Claire asked, surprised.

"A guess. Now tell us, before we freeze like icicles here in the snow." My flagging patience was nearly spent. "Young or old? What was he wearing?"

"He was sittin' in the fork of a big chestnut tree with a gun resting on his knees. I first presumed he was a hunter looking for game. Since he was on our land, I decided to ask him what he thought he was doing up there. I did ask, and there was no answer. As I tried to think what to do, he sat up, like he'd seen something in the distance." Claire's face lost any sheen of healthy color as she recited her story. "That's when I noticed I could kinda see through him. I saw the sky through his hat."

"Did you run away then?" Victoria asked.

"No," Claire whispered. "I couldn't move. He paid no mind to me, however. As if someone had called his name, he slipped down out of that tree, pulled his haversack onto his shoulders, picked up his rifle, and walked on."

After a few heartbeats of silence, Claire looked at me. "He was a soldier, Jules. One of ours."

"Oh, Clarey." Tears filled my eyes, for her fright and for feeling like I'd started something that had gotten out of hand like a brush fire. I put my arm around her and hugged her. "You don't need to be so afraid. Vee and I have seen them, too. I don't think they'll hurt us."

"I was so scared," Claire admitted again, and all I could think to do was to hold on to the living to fend off the dead.

And that's the way Sergeant Tacy found us. Three women in the middle of the day, sitting in the snow with their arms about each other like they might hide from the world.

The life nearly went out of me when he spoke.

"Might I enquire after the Oak Creek Plantation?"

The three of us jumped to our feet like scalded cats. We'd been so caught up in our own emotions, we'd lost track of the real world. I did manage to point the pistol in the right direction for once, though. And the man in question wisely raised his hands.

"I don't mean no harm, ladies," he said slowly. "I'm enquiring for Mrs. Julia Lovejoy." He'd already dismounted and the reins of his horse dangled from one hand. A mule was standing behind the horse, tethered to the saddle horn.

"I'm Mrs. Lovejoy," I said, but I didn't lower the pistol. "Who might you be?"

He smiled then and put his hands down without asking my permission. "I'm Sgt. Monroe Tacy, ma'am. We corresponded."

At that, I did lower the pistol. I ushered my sisters forward as best I could with a gun in my hand. When we were within two feet of Sergeant Tacy, I realized how unseemly all this must look to him. Our beautiful, placid, mannerly welcome had been spoiled, along with our dresses. On top of that, before I could introduce Claire and Victoria, Claire shot out a hand and poked Sergeant Tacy's arm. When she realized he was real and not a spirit she hid her reddening face by staring at his boots.

I could feel my own face growing warm even in the snowy air. He'd think we'd grown wild from neglect like the weeds in the rose garden. "You're younger than I expected," I said, I suppose to excuse myself for holding him under the gun. The truth was I had thought the Sergeant would be more William's age. But that was not the case.

"There's some of us that are young, and some like me, who only look young, ma'am. None who fought for three years can claim the former." He turned the subject then. "And who might these ladies be?" He slipped his soft felt hat from his head and smiled. He might not have done so if he'd known his grin framed by his mustache and trimmed beard made him look even younger. "Now let me guess. Would these be your sisters, Miss Victoria and Miss Claire?"

Surprised by his knowledge of my family, I had to bite back my questions. "Yes. This is, Victoria" — she nodded — "and Claire." Claire barely looked up, instead she dipped in a small curtsy.

"Well, I am very proud to finally meet you and to have arrived, by the Grace of the Almighty, on time." He hitched a thumb up, over his shoulder. "This mule balked so much I almost left him sittin' on the side of the road twice."

That portrait of stubbornness pushed us into action. Best to keep a mule moving until he got to where you wanted him to stop. We spent the next half hour settling Sergeant Tacy's horse and the reluctant mule in the barn. Claire filled a bucket with water for each animal, then when the Sergeant thanked her, she excused herself to tend to supper. I watched her go in puzzlement as I knew supper didn't need tending. But I shrugged off her skittishness and concurred as the Sergeant chose a corner of the loft for his sleeping quarters. He agreed with our assertion that the parson's room built into the northern side of the house just might be the coldest spot on Oak Creek Plantation.

As we left the barn, our visitor checked the hinges on the sagging door, perhaps worried that his newly purchased horse would push free and return whence he'd come. Not to mention what the mule may have planned. Our horse, Jeremiah, would have to be dragged off the property so we'd been lax with the repair. I offered to bring the Sergeant a hammer, and in very short order, the barn door was restored to its original upright condition.

I decided then and there that this visit of William's friend would bring us only good, and all the work we'd done in preparation was worth it.

Chapter Seven

Supper that evening was an enlightening affair. Sergeant Tacy turned out to be charming in his way and did his best to entertain us. After recounting once more his trial and mule tribulations on the trip north, Victoria stepped into the fray.

"And tell us, Sergeant, how your wife and family are willing to spare you for this arduous journey? Surely with you just back from the fighting, they must have needed time to adjust to your leaving again so soon."

Leave it to a true zealot to keep our purpose at heart and not lose sight of our plans.

"Please, ma'am, I would ask all you ladies to call me Monroe. I haven't been a Sergeant for months now, and since my daddy still walks the Earth, I've never felt much like a Mister." Then he answered Vee's question. "As for my family, you're right. My mother was het up about me going off again, but she finally came around." His eyes drifted to Claire. "I don't have a wife. Although now that I figure I might live to be older, I've been giving marriage some thought."

Victoria's gaze met mine across the table, and I could hear her association of ideas booming like a drummer's announcement, "Groom. Groom. Groom."

I got unaccountably nervous at our good fortune and changed the subject. "Tell us about being in the war, Ser— I mean, Monroe."

Monroe's expression changed subtly and for a moment he gave all his attention over to taking a sip of his coffee. In a fit of extravagance, we'd bought a small supply of expensive beans and parched them just for his visit. After replacing the cup carefully in the saucer he answered, "I expect there are some things I can tell you. But, honestly, most of it's not fit for a lady's ears."

He suddenly had Victoria's attention as well. "Tell us what you can," she said.

He nodded. Then he sat back in his chair and seemed to be looking toward an unseen horizon. He was right. In that moment he did *not* appear young. The "long gaze" sent a thrill of recognition through me. That look was the same as the ghostly soldiers we'd seen. The similarity made me itch to poke Monroe in the arm as Claire had done, to make sure we hadn't invited a spirit to our dinner table.

Then his expression softened and he looked . . . enraptured. As if he'd seen a sight that had touched his soul.

"I can tell you about the time I saw Robert Lee himself." He gestured toward the sideboard. "As close as from here to there." He sighed and shook his head, like the sight had been worth fighting a war for. "We'd been skirmishing for a day around Gettysburg, and full-fledged fightin' for another. We were thinning in numbers, backed up, stove in, and hardly able to stand for lack of water and a patch of shade. It was hot as hades. Pardon me, ma'am." He looked at me. "But your husband was there. Cussing Yanks with an officer's arsenal of swear words." He smiled. "The rest of us weren't so delicate."

My heart opened like a flower at the mention of William. Seeing the scene through Monroe Tacy's eyes made me feel for a moment as though William himself was sitting at the table, smiling fondly at his friend's story. I had to blink away the tears of my own rapture lest Monroe see them and stop talking.

"Anyway, we were yammering and complaining. Some were prayin' and others just sat there in a stupor.

"Then somebody yelled from down the line. Men started standing up and pointing." Monroe took a deep breath before smiling beatifically. "And there he was, General Robert Lee on his big white horse, comin' down the pike as calm as you please. He'd pulled off his hat and clasped it to his breast." Monroe held up his hands like he was gesturing for quiet, although none of us but him had uttered a word. "The closer he got, the quieter the men got. Like his mere presence could soothe the hearts of thousands of those suffering and fearful. I saw soldiers, old and young alike, with tears streaming down their faces — not from pain — but for the love of that old man. It was a sight, truth to tell.

"And your husband, ma'am. He made me help him up. He stood straight and tall even though by that point he'd taken the shot in the thigh. And when General Lee drew near, Lieutenant Lovejoy saluted him. And you know what? The old man saluted him back. Both of us I suppose, since I was standing next to William." Monroe slapped his hand on the table making me jump. "A damned sight," he said again. "One I'll never forget."

Then he realized he'd been crude. "Sorry, ladies," he apologized, looking each of us in the eye. He then returned his more serious attention to me. "You know what Lieutenant Lovejoy said to me on that day, which turned out to be his final one on this Earth? He said, 'I'd die for that old man.' Meaning Robert Lee. And, I suppose the Yanks took him at his word, as did I."

I wasn't sure what to make of William's declaration, although hearing it did not surprise me. I'd known of my husband's commitment to the cause early on and had supported it. I only wished I'd been better prepared for the outcome of such devotion.

"Thank you, Monroe, for telling me — us. Wives in a war are so often without any news of their loved ones. I cannot tell you how much it means to hear from someone who actually stood with William on that fateful day. And for you to come so far on this errand is a true blessing."

Monroe ducked his head briefly. "I need to thank you ladies for offering your hospitality."

Victoria spoke to fill an awkward moment. "Speaking of hospitality . . . Claire? We've forgotten about our pie. Serg— I mean, Monroe, would you care for a piece

96

of vinegar pie and another cup of coffee?" I'm sure she knew he would, since he'd eaten supper like he was facing his last meal. There was little doubt that we had not plumbed the bottom of Monroe's capacity for food.

"Yes ma'am," Monroe said and grinned, erasing the hardships of war from his expression. After Claire and Victoria left the table, he turned to me. "I intend to carry out my errand this evening, ma'am, when you and I have an opportunity to speak alone. But first, if you don't mind, I'd like to distribute some things my mother sent along for your use."

"That will be fine." Truth be told I was in no hurry to revisit William's actual demise. Just seeing him, alive in my mind's eye, saluting Robert E. Lee was close enough for right now.

After supper and two pieces of pie, as promised, Monroe went out to the barn and retrieved several parcels, which had traveled atop the reluctant mule. As he stacked the items into a pile on the floor, he suddenly seemed unsure.

"My mother, after coming to terms with me making this journey, made up a list of things that you ladies might need." He rubbed the whiskers at his chin as if he was searching for words. "She said that way out in the middle of —" He stopped, his skin darkening above his collar.

"Nowhere?" I offered solicitously.

He nodded. "She meant no harm. Anyway, because we live in a port city, we're able to buy more with less money. She thought I might as well bring this to you."

When we simply sat and waited for him to continue, he picked up one of the three larger packages and handed it to me. "I don't know what goes with what or to whom." Like a reluctant Kris Kringle, he handed the next to Claire. "You all will have to fight amongst yourselves."

Half an hour later I wanted to kiss Monroe's mother, and possibly his father as well. I might have even gone out to the barn and kissed the mule that had carried our bounty, but the sun had already gone down, and I did not believe the mule would be impressed. When all was said and done, we were the proud owners of four bolts of new cloth, two winter and two summer; three pairs of serviceable kid shoes in almost the correct sizes; buttons and notions for the dresses we would make; a current issue of *Peterson's Women's Magazine*; and one fashion plate doll to which Claire clung as if it might float out the front door without the proper attention.

It was the finest imitation Christmas we'd ever experienced.

The smile on Victoria's face said it all, but she found the need to speak just the same. The result was more of a volley than an exchange. "This is such a wonderful surprise. Mr. Tacy, you are without a doubt from a fine family. How can we ever repay you? I hope you'll convey the heartfelt gratitude of my sisters and myself to your mother for her thoughtfulness. If you would give me her address, I'll be delighted to write and thank her myself."

Monroe again shifted his feet. "I suspect it takes a woman to know what a woman wants," he said. "I can see you're happy with her choices. I'll make sure she knows it."

Victoria and Claire each gathered an armload of the gifts to take them upstairs. That left me alone briefly with Sergeant Tacy. The room seemed overly quiet without the excited discussion of who would have what dress out of which cloth. I knew I could not delay Monroe's mission any longer, but first I wanted to make sure he understood what he'd accomplished without trying.

"Monroe, I'd like to thank you again." He shook his head and started to speak. I stopped him. "I know, your mother sent those gifts to us, but you had to carry them a long way, and deal with a troublesome mule in the bargain. Another might have refused, or left the extra weight behind at the first sign of it being too much of a burden.

"I thank you in the most part for my sisters rather than me. For you have already done more than you needed in my cause. I can never repay you properly for that."

Sergeant Tacy sat on the edge of the chair closest to mine. I knew by the look on his face it was time for me to accept William's token. I drew in a deep breath, smoothed my third-best dress's skirts and looked him in the eye. "Tell me what happened to my husband."

He swallowed once, then looked down as if to gather his words. Then he met my gaze again and looked pleasant, as if the news he would impart wasn't all that bad. "First, ma'am, you have to know that I stuck to your husband like a deer tick in high water. Lieutenant Lovejoy was an honest officer who treated his men fairly. He always made sure that if there were food or supplies anywhere within ten miles, his men had some of it. Or, he'd dang well know why. On more than one occasion he persuaded a farmer into contributing more than he might have otherwise, either through fine words or the show of his pistol.

"We also knew when things got tough we could depend on him to not send us headlong into hell without any hope of surviving the day.

"My job in the company was to listen to what needed to be done and make sure the men did it. In battle, I pretty much always kept your husband in sight. No use winning a skirmish if your officers are taken down."

Monroe's face changed, and I readied myself for painful news.

"At Gettysburg, things were all topsy-turvy. Nothin' we did seemed to work right."

He stopped speaking, and swallowed once. I thought he might need a glass of water. I made to get up. "Would you —"

"No," he answered and indicated for me to remain in my chair.

I settled back and waited. It was then, sitting close, that I noticed the line of a scar over his left brow running from his forehead into his hair. The war had marked him in a more direct way than it had marked me, yet I knew neither of us would ever be the same.

"I don't know how many men died that day," he said with that distant look returning to his eyes. "I know at our position we went in with over two thousand fit for fighten' and came out with less than eight hundred. The killin' was an awful thing to see.

"Your husband, as I told you before, had already taken some Yank artillery metal to his thigh. Not much to do about that since the wound was high and deep. Going to the surgeon would only mean gettin' carved up worse. When we were called upon again to move, he had me help him limp forward. He'd lost his horse the day before." Monroe shook his head. "I didn't know then that William had already decided he'd die on the field. At his instruction I left him standing propped against a tree while I did my best to carry out his orders. And he stood there, calm as you please, watching over his men as bullets cut leaves from the branches above him and splintered the wood of his only protection.

"But it was the artillery that took him."

Monroe looked me in the eye, and I

could have sworn I saw a sheen of tears. "And you may change your good opinion of me when I tell you that your husband died saving my miserable life." He blinked back the moisture in his eyes, and I kept my gaze steady although I could feel my hands clenched into fists. Not in anger at this man, but in fury at the sheer wastefulness of war. All the lives taken and others ruined in the process. Somehow, however, I found my voice.

"I assure you, Sergeant Tacy, I do not hold you responsible for my husband's decisions. He must have valued your friendship, and that is something I will not deride."

"Ma'am, I'm not sure it was my friendship he valued, although I believe that was part of it. You see, soldiers in battle, especially officers, are trained to do what's best for the engagement. What I mean is, I think Lieutenant Lovejoy knew he could not recover from his wound, and he knew the company needed me as an officer with battle experience. So when the shells and grapeshot came in, and I got in the way, he did what was best for his men. He left his protection and pushed me down, falling over me. It should have been me what died." Monroe stopped speaking then for a full minute. I took the time to pull my handkerchief from my belt and wipe away my own tears. When both of us were more composed, Sergeant Tacy went on.

"I dragged him back to cover, ma'am, and tried to staunch his wounds. That's when he set me upon this errand which has brought me to you." Monroe cleared his throat, unbuttoned the top button of his shirt and drew a gold chain over his head. A gold ring glinted in the lamplight as he handed it to me. I recognized William's wedding ring.

"Lieutenant Lovejoy bade me give this to you and tell you he is forever grateful to God that you became his wife. He said he wished he could have had many more years at your side."

I stared at William's ring resting in the palm of my hand, feeling both full and empty at the same time. Empty because of all the losses of the past including my own ring which I'd sold, and full because my husband had sent his token of our marriage with a last message of his love. Yes, I'd been fearsome proud to be William's wife. But, being William's widow took a bit more strength. I rested my free hand lightly on Monroe's.

"I'm sure William knew what he was

about when he saved you, Sergeant Tacy. And, do not shrug off the depths of his friendship, for he was not always a man of war. Those he loved, he loved well. The fact that you have fulfilled your promise to him exemplifies the potential he saw in you." I had to swallow back the growing lump in my throat, determined not to make Monroe feel worse than he did already. There would be time later for tears. "I realize this must've been a burden. Please know I am grateful, and I release you from any further responsibility on my part."

The words sounded colder than I'd intended, but just then I couldn't find any warmth within. The ring lay warm in my hand, but the bitter realities of war had nearly frozen my blood. With the image of William dying in a bloody killing field flooding my mind, I stood.

"I believe I will go upstairs now," I said. "You may take the lamp to find your way to the barn. We will look for you at breakfast tomorrow."

"Yes, ma'am," Monroe said and stood as well.

He waited for me to turn the corner into the main hallway before picking up the lamp. The dim shadows were shifting around me when I felt an arm slide about my waist. I was too emotional to start at the suddenness of the touch.

"Oh, Jules," Victoria whispered as she hugged me to her. "I'm so, so, sorry. Perhaps it is better not to know." She was weeping, and I realized she must have been standing in the hallway, in the dark, listening to the details of William's demise. "I couldn't help but listen. I hope you can forgive me."

I hugged her closer, not in the least bit angry. We'd shared so much. If she could stand to hear the truth then I would not deprive her of it. "My legs feel like unsteady posts in shifting ground. If you'll help me up these stairs, I'll forgive you anything. I would like to find my bed and close my eyes on this day."

With Victoria's strong arm supporting me, we made our way up the stairs.

The dream was different this time. The stuff of distant nightmares brought home to roost in my mind. I found myself in the middle of a terrible battle, cringing when the cannons boomed, looking for William, looking for a place to hide. Hoping for a familiar face. And all the while men raced by me without acknowledging my presence or my screams of fear. Instead of being

106

surprised to find a woman dressed in her nightclothes among them, they seemed unable to see me. I'd become the ghost in their world. I tossed and turned through the mud and the blood of battle after battle until near dawn when the very real sound of far-off gunfire woke me from my fitful sleep.

Chapter Eight

I dressed as quickly as I could and met Victoria in the hall. Claire came out of her room still in her gown as we were descending the stairs. "We're going to get the sergeant. Get dressed but stay in the house," I told her.

The deep orange of sunrise was just candling the tops of the oaks as we left the house and hurried to the barn. I knocked on the barn door soundly, not knowing what protocol to use for entering our own barn when it had become guest quarters. There was no reply or movement inside.

"Sergeant Tacy?" I knew he'd instructed us to call him by his given name, but in this time of emergency, I felt a great deal more comforted by using his military rank. "Are you there? Did you hear the shots?"

Again, no answer.

We took matters into our own hands and opened the latch. Victoria swung the door closed behind us as I headed toward the dim corner the Sergeant had chosen for his resting place.

"Sergeant?" I called again, but as I got closer I could see that his blankets had been folded. He'd left some time earlier. His horse nickered softly, hoping for a bit of charity, no doubt. Then I noticed the mule was gone.

"You don't suppose he went riding off on that mule do you?"

"And leave a perfectly willing horse behind? I doubt it," Victoria declared.

Defeated, we both turned to go back to the house. As usual, whatever needed facing, we would do it alone and together. After donning a few more layers of warm clothes, we set Claire to stoking the fire in the cookhouse and beginning breakfast while Victoria and I circled the house several times, searching the horizon in each direction for any signs of trouble.

Victoria had recently defected from guard duty to cooking out of fear that Claire would burn the biscuits, when I spied Sergeant Tacy. He and his mule were coming in from the east. I couldn't see his cargo, but I noticed Monroe was limping. And, he had a rifle slung over his shoulder. Thinking he'd been shot, I rushed to the cookhouse and told my sisters to put on a kettle of water to boil for bandages, then I hurried out to meet him.

"What in the world happened?" I questioned, out of breath from running. Then before he could answer, I saw the deer draped across the mule's back.

"Keep walking while we talk, ma'am, or this mule might dump his cargo one more time and I'll have to end him right here."

Finding my breath and coming to my senses I began to catalog more of the scene before me. Serg— Monroe's hat was crushed, and he had a bloody scrape on his arm where his shirt had been ripped. And, like I said, he was favoring his right foot.

"After serving with some of the best pack animals a soldier could hope for, I had to buy one as sour as a green persimmon."

"Were those gunshots yours?"

"Yes, ma'am," he answered. "I thought you ladies could use some fresh meat to smoke or dry for the winter. As long as I'm your guest, I feel I should provide what I can." He shook his head, disgusted. "But I should have shot the mule and made the deer haul *him* back." He gave the animal in peril a dark look. "When I tried to tie down the buck, that mule went bone-jarrin' crazy. I almost lost him altogether,

110

which would have been all right if I wasn't as stubborn as he is."

Monroe raised his bloody arm and ripped shirt. "Look what he's done to my shirt. And my toes . . . If I get this boot off and find some broken toes, I'll —" He stopped himself midthreat. "Have you ever cooked mule, ma'am?"

I almost laughed, but at that moment the mule must have either divined Monroe's thoughts or he smelled something resembling home because he picked up the pace, practically leading his master rather than the other way around. We had to hurry to keep up.

Monroe insisted on dressing out the deer before he had breakfast or sat down to have his wounds tended. Later as we fussed over him, his mood improved although his intentions toward the mule remained fixed.

"Is there someone hereabouts that you don't particularly like who might buy that mule from me?" he asked as he sat swathed in my mother's rose tree quilt while Victoria stitched the tear in his shirt and I cleaned his mule battle wounds. Claire sat in the corner of the cookhouse with her hands folded in her lap. She'd silently served him a plate of breakfast be-

111

fore retreating to her perch.

"I suppose there are many around here who could use a good mule," I offered, but I couldn't think of one I'd burden with Monroe's mule.

"Well, that good part rules them out, I suppose," he said with a half smile. He glanced toward Claire as if to see her enjoyment of his humor. When she noticed his attention, though, she looked down.

It startled me to see my sister act in such a meek manner. I determined to speak to her later about it. I gave Monroe's scrape a final washing and dropped the cloth back into the hot water.

"I suppose it's time we looked at those toes,"

I said.

"No, ma'am. I mean, I'll take care of it," Monroe said. "You ladies have done enough. Besides, I'm of a mind to leave my boot on until the swelling goes down. Otherwise, I won't be able to get it back on." He smiled up at me. "Too cold to be walking in bare feet."

"That's true. But I don't like the idea of your foot going putrid because you didn't want to pull off your boot." I looked at my younger sister. "Claire? Go up to Papa's wardrobe and bring one of his house boots — for the right foot."

With a nod instead of a word, Claire disappeared into the house.

"This might be a bit too distressing for her," Monroe volunteered.

So, he had noticed her shyness as well. "Yes, it might be. It's been awhile since it was more than just the three of us to worry about. I'll send her out before we examine your foot."

"It might be too distressing for you as well."

Now that surprised me. This man who had already told me in great detail the bloody wartime truth of my husband's death thought I would grow faint at the sight of his damaged foot. In the past he might have been right, but too much unruly water had passed under the current bridge of my life. One smashed foot wouldn't bring me down.

"I have helped bring a neighbor's child into the world when there was no one else to come. If you think tending to your foot could be worse or more bloody than that, you are wrong." I heard Victoria's soft inhale of breath behind me and saw Monroe's shocked reaction at my bold words mixed with the typical male terror of the delivery process. If he could speak of war and the end of life, then I could speak of birth and the beginning.

His expression shifted as if he could discern my indignation. I should have taken it as a warning of things to come. "Well then," he said, "I stand corrected and firmly put in my place. If you have a hankering to stare at my old hairy toes then I won't stop you."

That brought my color up. I had no more interest in his toes than any doctor, and he knew it. He was deviling me, and it worked. I was saved from undue suffering by Claire's return. As I handed the boot to Monroe so he could compare the size to his own, spoke to her. "Claire, why don't you go on in and start measuring out the cloth for that new dress you need?" It was my signal to remind her of our plans to go to Savannah. It took her only a few seconds to catch on, and her eyes lit with more enthusiasm.

"Are you sure you don't need me?" she asked, her gaze again fixed on Monroe's boots rather than anywhere else in the room.

"I'm sure," I answered. "This shouldn't take long."

Claire nodded and left the warmth of the kitchen for the house.

I couldn't tell if the Sergeant's toes were broken or not. Two of them were swollen and bluish and a third had a scrape. He insisted on cleaning them the best he could, then Victoria and I helped him stand to get his foot into my father's house boot.

It looked rather strange. "I'm sorry we don't have a leather boot to offer. We sent off all of Papa's usable clothes to the war effort. We only held back the things which would be of little use to a soldier."

Monroe declared it perfect since the bigger, softer boot gave his toes enough room for him to walk normally. "Well, this ought to do just fine," he said as he stared down at his two mismatched feet. "Now I won't be hobbled. I intended to carve a slab of venison to cook for supper tonight. Shall I bring it in or build a pit?"

At the promise of slow-roasted venison, Victoria and I both concurred. "A pit," we said at once.

Looking like a man with a purpose, Monroe nodded and left to accomplish the task.

As Victoria and I returned to the house, we found Claire gazing out of the window. When she noticed us, she turned and busied herself with the material she'd unrolled but which lay uncut. When I glanced out of the same window, I saw Monroe gathering wood for the cooking fire. Claire came back to stand next to me.

"How long will he stay?" she asked.

I couldn't fathom her hopes or fears, only her question. It was one I'd considered myself.

"I don't know. We haven't discussed it. I had assumed such a trip would demand a rest of at least a week. But being a former soldier may have accustomed him to traveling at a harder pace. Though," I added, "since he injured his foot, he might remain here longer." Then I attempted to take a tally of her feelings on the subject. After all, the sergeant had mentioned being a bachelor, a rare commodity in these times. Something we had all wished for. "Would you like for him to stay longer?"

"It'll take at least two weeks to make our new dresses. Don't you think? We couldn't leave for Savannah before then."

So, this was more about going to Savannah than about finding a husband. I glanced toward Victoria in consternation. She shook her head.

"Then we should begin working right now and see how much time two dresses require."

So we put aside the nearly finished wedding dress and between the three of us, the first day dress, for Claire, took a week. Much had changed on Oak Creek Plantation in that time. January had given way to February and our houseguest looked to be no closer to leaving. Monroe recovered from his tussle with the mule and now walked in his own boots without a limp. He had taken it upon himself to hammer and haul, fix and replace anything he came upon that needed attention. In private, Victoria and I vowed not to be caught outside the house in a shabby condition lest our industrious Monroe set to refurbishing the human occupants of Oak Creek.

I only wished we could interest Claire in venturing out.

Not that she needed fixing. I just didn't understand her reaction to Sergeant Tacy. She'd been so brokenhearted at the thought of never meeting a husband. As far as I could discern, Monroe Tacy was of sound limb and mind, his sense of the ridiculous was seasoned by a level of intelligence. He was relatively young, certainly a few seasons younger than myself, which should have pleased our sister, yet living through the war had made him serious. We could hardly help but see his ambition and industriousness while tripping over new porch steps and closing doors that actually kept the cold wind on the other side.

We, of course, had refrained from mentioning our marriage plot to Monroe. I determined once more to speak firmly with Claire about her true intentions when I returned from accompanying Monroe into town. We were set on buying some new hardware for the harnesses and the plow. Whatever pieces I felt we could afford, since Monroe had convinced me that spring would arrive again this year and our fields would require planting. We, meaning the full-time residents of Oak Creek Plantation, were dangerously close to having to beg for credit from Mr. Tate — a situation my father would have abhorred. Another point I kept from the industrious Sergeant.

As I stepped out of our newly refurbished front door, I found Monroe leaning against our wagon, waiting for me.

"It's a great pleasure to get into a wagon pulled by a horse I haven't had to harness," I said, as I allowed Monroe to help me up.

He went around, stepped up, then cocked his head toward our horse. "Are you sure this old tower of hair and bones will make it into town?"

"There's more to Jeremiah than he

seems," I scolded. "Besides —" I folded my hands primly, "— if he were any more of a horse he would not have tolerated the unintentional abuse of being left in the care of three women. Go on, Jeremiah," I instructed, and out of habit the old horse moved off.

"Tell me, what are your plans when you return to Savannah?" I asked. I had all the way to town to get what I really wanted to know — how long he would be with us and if he was a true husband candidate.

Monroe shrugged and kept his eyes on the road. "Well, my family didn't fare as poorly as many during the war. My brothers worked with my father to keep the business going in all but the worst times toward the end. Even the blockades couldn't shut their doors." He gave Jeremiah an absentminded tap with the reins. Jeremiah prudently ignored him. "They would like for me to join them," he said.

"So, you'll go back, take your place in the family business and settle down."

"Maybe, ma'am. I just don't know yet. I've spent three years traipsin' between Savannah, Richmond, and points beyond. I'm not in a hurry to be a shopkeeper next to my brother."

"What of your heart? Don't you have a

sweetheart back home?" The memory of Victoria's frown made my face warm. For the life of me I couldn't remember when or how I'd become so bold.

Monroe looked at me then. I thought for a moment he'd just ignore my rude question. But slowly, he smiled. "I appreciate your concern, Mrs. Lovejoy. I imagine a woman like yourself, who knows what love is about, would worry over a sad soul such as me. But, no, I have no sweetheart pining for me. The only girl I'd ever been sweet on up and married another fella while I was off warrin'. I don't blame her none. We probably wouldn't have suited each other anyhow." His smile blossomed into a grin. "I believe my heart remains intact, just where I left it."

In the face of his humor, I smiled in return. I'd done my duty. I'd found out what we needed to know before Victoria and I set ourselves on the course of convincing Monroe, and, at this point Claire as well, that they could make a good match.

"How long were you thinking of staying at Oak Creek?"

"Again, I'd say that depends on the generosity of you ladies, and your patience, I suppose. Truth be told, it feels good to be building and fixing things rather than tearing them down or blowing them up."

Or killing them. The words seemed to hang in the air.

"We appreciate the work you've been doing, Monroe. But we don't wish to take advantage of you."

The grin returned. "Ma'am, I promise I will speak up if I feel overburdened. Besides, I feel the need to work for my keep. In case you haven't noticed, I've been enjoying the bounty of your table."

Another thing I had on my list, provisions. I only hoped I could afford to feed our newly self-appointed field hand regardless of the deer he'd killed.

We let the conversation lapse into small talk about the weather, crops and such until we reached Stoneman. It hadn't occurred to me that I should be prepared for anything. I didn't see the danger of the figurative cannon until the ball had fallen among us, and I had introduced Monroe to Mr. Tate at the mercantile.

"Oh," Mr. Tate responded. "You must be Miss Claire's intended."

"Well, I —" Monroe began, then looked to me for clarification.

Before I could think, Mr. Tate rattled on. "Yes, it'll be good to see two young people making a new start." His gaze sharpened on Monroe. "Miss Claire said you fought for the cause."

"Yes, sir, with the 24th," Monroe had the presence of mind to say as Mr. Tate pumped his hand two more times for good measure.

"It's darn good to meet you. Anyone who served under the battle flag of Virginia is welcome here."

"Thank you, sir."

Mr. Tate thumped Monroe on the back. "I'm lookin' forward to the weddin' in March."

Now this is when I found out how truly well-mannered Mr. Monroe Tacy could be in a pinch. He followed my lead and completely ignored the reference to him being Claire's intended. Either he was waiting for me to set the storekeeper right, or he hadn't heard the man's proclamation correctly. I had already surmised that Monroe's hearing was excellent. So his act of discretion could only be for my benefit.

Unfortunately, it put me in a difficult position when he insisted on paying the bill for our purchases and even signing a letter of credit on our behalf. I had to wait until we were on the road home to take him to task about it.

"Mr. Tacy, are you a wealthy man?"

"Ma'am, I asked you to call me Monroe. And, no, I'm not a particularly wealthy man, although not a poor one either."

After laying what I thought was a fine trap, I asked, "Then how do you suppose my sisters and I repay you for what you have paid out in our behalf?"

"I don't suppose nothin', ma'am. What little I spend while I'm with you would never be enough to repay your husband for my life. Mere money can't cancel a debt of life and death."

That put my argument at a disadvantage. As I was searching for another way to explain that he was not responsible for us, he moved into other territories. "Who is Miss Claire marrying in the spring?"

I paid great attention to the action of smoothing my skirts as the wagon creaked along. I hoped for a brilliant, laudable way to explain Mr. Tate's assumption, but again I was denied any divine wisdom.

"We don't know, exactly," I answered honestly.

Monroe turned to look at me then. I suppose he'd just begun to wonder about the sanity of the three women he'd been visiting. "What does that mean?"

Again, I had to give him credit for not leaping to conclusions or assumptions. For not deciding and then informing me what he thought. Unfortunately, that meant he was going to force me to explain it to him.

"Well . . ." I tried to smile harmlessly and with a little dignity since this would most likely be the last time he looked to me for any explanation. But my smile faded. I couldn't think of one good lie that would cover what had been occurring at Oak Creek the prior two months.

"Victoria and I intend to see Claire married," I said.

When I didn't elaborate he prodded, "Yes, I understand that. But to whom? And where is he?"

"What do you mean, where is he? Why of course, he's off as you say warrin' and will return in the spring." I hoped that would suffice as an explanation.

"Beggin' your pardon, Mrs. Lovejoy, but any soldier who fought for the cause should have been back home long before now. What news do you have from him?"

I stared at Monroe's hands, firmly holding Jeremiah's reins and scoured my memory for a proper response. Could I mention a post in the wilderness? Could I expound on the marriage of politics and men of war that called them to other arenas for battle? Or could I just say we'd had a letter three weeks prior and he would be home soon? That's when my divine help kicked in. I folded my own hands in my lap and did my best to appear honest.

"That's the problem. There's been no news of him." He frowned at me and started to speak, but I spoke first. "I know what that means. It means he's most probably . . ."

"Dead," Monroe finished for me.

"Well, yes. We'd thought of that, Victoria and I. But we have not been able to bring ourselves to speak of it to Claire. She's so young and . . ."

Monroe watched Jeremiah's progress for a long time before he spoke again. "I'm sorry to hear that, ma'am. I truly am. If there's anything more I can do, please enlighten me."

My sister the zealot would have decreed this as the perfect moment to broach the subject of the trip to Savannah. Unfortunately, my conscience was at war with my faith in our enterprise. I felt truly despicable for lying to an honorable man and then wheedling him into a trip. I resolved to let events rest for the moment and later, if we could see no other way to accomplish our goal, I would set Victoria on him.

I had just begun to feel better about my duplicitous answers when staid, stick-in-the-mud Jeremiah sidestepped like a colt. As I glanced up, I divined the reason and felt of the same mind.

Thirty yards up the road I could see two men, one sitting and one leaning along the fence row. I casually glanced sideways at Monroe to see if he'd noticed. His face was set in the same frown that had formed over hearing the bad news about Claire's intended. I could see no change or curiosity directed at the two strangers.

As we moved closer, Jeremiah pulled as best he could toward the opposite side of the road. But Monroe didn't seem to be paying any attention to him. Each plodding step brought us nearer and, as always, once I saw these spirits, I could not draw my regard from them.

There could be no mistaking that these were Confederates, with or without a flag. The one on the ground was a weathered graybeard, who'd probably been soldiering most of his life. He reclined with his cap draped on one drawn-up knee, his bedroll supporting him. The other soldier was younger, wearing a new slouch hat at a rakish angle, but the rest of him was wiry and battle-worn just the same. He busied himself filling a cup from a canteen. As we drew abreast of them, the younger handed the cup to the older then looked up at me — at us — as if he might call out a hello. The entire tableau shimmered, beginning to disappear.

Emboldened by my companion's presence, I wanted so badly to speak, to ask them why they were still wandering the roads and what we could do to help them get home. But, after nearly losing possession of one of our family's secrets to Monroe, I couldn't divulge the other — the fact that we appeared to be downright plagued with Confederate soldiers who seemed less than completely dead.

Monroe remained blessedly silent, although when I studied him, his color seemed to be up, as if he wore his emotions like a flag. I assumed he was still wrestling with the fact that he had survived, while so many others had died. Surely if he'd seen the spirits, he would have spoken.

"Are you well?" I asked.

He nodded rather curtly and made a great show of guiding Jeremiah back into the tracks in the middle of the road. I determined to let it go.

Then Monroe said, "I expect those two were from Texas. Those ol' boys have a certain look about 'em. Their battle yell could afright Lucifer himself."

Chapter Nine

"You saw them?" I scarcely breathed.

"Saw who?" he said with a complete lack of expression.

My indignation rose then. "You know perfectly well *who*," I practically huffed. "The present is not the time for playing the fool."

He shrugged and his mouth twisted with a wry smile. "You're wrong, ma'am. Many times playing the fool is the only way to survive."

My outrage flagging, I drew in a calming breath. In his way he was telling me all was well. The world around us remained solid and real, from road to horse and wagon, to sky. Monroe himself appeared as calm as a pond stone. So I determined I should follow suit. After all, this wasn't the first time I'd seen the lost souls of the war. The difference being that this time I had an unbiased witness. I wanted to learn more.

"Have you seen them before?" I asked.

"The spirits, I mean."

Monroe's features settled into that long, unwavering, soldier gaze. The wagon creaked to the rhythm of Jeremiah's plodding steps, but everything else seemed hushed. "Now and again," he answered. "More so during the war. Especially after we'd been through a hard fight. They walk the battlefield, searching for their comrades. Not knowing the war is over for them I s'pose.

"Once one of my messmates offered a plate of corn mush to a stray Alabama regular who was leaning against a tree near our fire, whittlin'. The man smiled his thanks then promptly disappeared.

"A sight like that can be unnerving while you're waiting for the war to break around you again. Death behind you, all around, and marchin' in come the next smoky dawn."

The thought gave me a bone-deep chill. "I don't know how anyone survived it."

"That's a puzzlement to me as well. We never knew who would fall, no matter the sign or the luck. In a way, it made facing the guns easier. We knew our fate was out of our hands. We were there to fight with honor for God and Robert Lee and to take whatever comes." Monroe sighed and shook his head sadly. "It's bad luck that all three of you ladies lost your men in the war. Bad luck for sure."

My guilt redoubled at his words. I'd allowed him to believe a lie, now I didn't know how to call it back. "I'm hoping Claire will fare well since she has not been —" I wanted to say in love but that sounded frivolous. Everyone in the county expected her to marry a man in the spring and they would assume love to be involved at some level. We were not royalty who married perfect strangers. As Monroe turned the wagon into our drive, I was still searching for words.

"You mean she's young and she could love again?"

"That is my fervent hope," I replied, allowing Monroe to provide me with an escape.

"That is the sum of what any of us can hope," he said with an air of finality.

With all the talk of spirits and death that day, I had let the opportunity to quiz Monroe further and more specifically on his plans pass. He himself hadn't seen fit to enlighten me. I should have known I could depend on Victoria.

That evening, as we sat down to supper,

Monroe made a special effort to comment on the table since Victoria had mentioned Claire had done the lion's share of the work. He also asked Claire about the progress of her second new dress. After Claire had given him short, although civil replies, Victoria waded into the fray.

"So, Monroe, exactly how long do you plan to visit with us?"

I picked up my water glass to hide my agitation. This lying business had too many hidden traps for me to feel confident. I drew in a deep breath and took a sip.

"Why, I thought I would stay on a month or so and get this place back in shape by the time Miss Claire's intended arrives. It'll be my wedding present to the family."

I found breathing deeply and drinking water at the same instant doesn't serve a body well. I nearly choked to death in front of all of them. As Victoria pounded between my shoulders, I coughed and kept my watery gaze on Monroe. What was he about? He knew Claire's intended wasn't coming back — we'd both decided on that probability. I should, however, have kept an eye on Claire, because in the excitement, she fled the room.

As soon as I regained my breath, I excused myself and followed her, leaving Victoria to entertain Monroe. I found Claire in her room, settled into a chair bristling with a posture of rebellion.

"Claire? What in the world is the matter with you?" I rarely took her to task, but in this instance I was determined to know what she was up to and determined to know quickly. "How could you be so rude as to leave the supper table in such a fashion?"

Claire simply stared at me for a moment. I suppose she was surprised by my tone of voice. Her mulish expression hadn't changed, however.

"He's staying for a *month*," she said finally, making the last word sound like a curse. "What difference does it make if I have new dresses if I can't go to Savannah?"

That's when I recognized that somewhere along the way, we, Victoria and I — I would not accuse my parents — must have spoiled Claire. Or raised her hopes beyond common sense. In that moment, it came to me that this was ultimately my fault. Victoria had thrown her heart into the scheme to give Claire what she wanted, but it had been my invention. I had no idea how to avert the obvious derailment of our venture.

"Claire, Monroe has been a godsend to us in many ways. If he's willing to help us beyond what he has already done, then I will not allow you to treat him with such bad manners.

"As for your trip to Savannah, you will be very fortunate if you have the opportunity at all, so a delay of one month should not be so devastating. And, you should think ahead. If you act like a spoiled child who's been thwarted, perhaps Monroe will come to the conclusion you are too much trouble to accompany."

Or to marry.

It was a downright shame that Claire could not see any possibilities in our guest. My curiosity, prodded by my anger, led me to ask, "What is it you don't like about Monroe?"

Her rebellion evaporated then. She folded her hands and locked her gaze on them. "I don't know."

"That's not good enough Claire." I pushed. "What is it you find offensive?"

She remained silent, and I waited, unwilling to give her my guesses so she might choose one without looking to her own heart for the answer. It was a contest that proved the bond of our blood, for we each seemed as stubborn as the other. I, however, had had a few more years to perfect my tactics. I began the rhythmic tapping of my foot.

Finally, with a sigh she gave in. "He scares me."

I hadn't thought she could surprise me, but she had. In my estimation there wasn't one tittle or jot about Monroe Tacy to arouse fear. He was straightforward and tenderhearted in his ways.

"What has he done that scares you?" I asked.

My tone must have worried her, because she answered immediately, "Nothing. Not really. It's just the way he looks at me sometimes. His eyes remind me of the ghost in the tree."

All of a sudden, I had the truth of it. At least I thought I had the truth. I remembered that my sister had no great experience with men in the manner of courting or even of friendship. The last four years had curtailed most social contact, and those would have been her years to get her footing when dealing with men as a woman, not as a young girl. She needed to learn which looks were harmless and which she should scorn. In my estimation, Monroe Tacy was the perfect man to practice on.

I sat down on the bed and indicated for Claire to come sit next to me. I put my arm around her and hugged her close.

"Now Claire, you must take my word there is nothing to fear from Monroe. He's not a spirit or a coward without honor. He's a man, and although men have their strengths, they also have their weaknesses. I'm sure he looks at you because you are a vision, and he enjoys your lovely face." I didn't mention that he also probably felt terrible because he believed she'd lost her intended in the war. "Besides, as you know, we have had a very lonely and tragic four years since the war began. Think how Monroe feels, having to leave his home to fight and watch his friends die. You must have some sympathy for that."

"I do," Claire mumbled.

"Well then, I'd like you to promise me something. I'd like you to promise to try to make friends with Monroe. I'm sure you'll feel much better when you know him and see he means us only well." I lifted her chin to look into her eyes. "Will you do that for me?"

She nodded, looking properly chastised. I only hoped the feeling would last.

"Now, let's go back down, make our apologies, and finish supper."

★ ★ ★

"She's afraid of him," I said to Victoria as I fed small twigs into the stove to replenish the fire the next morning. Claire had set out on her usual morning chores leaving Victoria and me time to discuss what was to be done.

"I feel as though our prayers have been answered," I continued. "But that our prayers and Claire's appear to be different in content."

Victoria didn't speak immediately. She gave her complete attention to filling the kettle. Earlier I had provided her a full report about the previous day, from Mr. Tate's incorrect assumption, to Monroe and me seeing the spirits on the road home. But now we had to discuss a different thread in our ever growing web — Claire's reluctance. I had the fire fed to a crackling blaze by the time she replied.

"Sometimes the idea of a thing is more enticing than the actual fulfillment," she said. "Especially when one is young and naive."

"That predicament affects the not-so-young as well," I agreed, thinking along another vein. Going off to fight for your principles, your state's rights, and your heroes, seems romantic and enticing in the heat of the moment and in the safety of your home. But after what Monroe had described of war, and after the many tragedies I had seen overtaking us and our neighbors, I believe we would have been better served to solve our differences in another way. Ideals be damned.

"We need to find some method of bringing back the happier times," Victoria went on, oblivious to my decidedly unhappy thoughts. "If we could attend a picnic or a dance, some kind of social where Claire and Monroe, where all of us could relax and smile and get to know each other, I believe it could be different."

My treacherous memory produced images of a time when things were happier. When I had been as carefree as a spring foal in summer pastures. When I had been in love with William and he with me. We'd attended every picnic and made our own when faced with vacant time. We'd danced and laughed under the same sun and moon I now walked under alone. I had to fight the seductive lure of the past; it was the present I needed to face.

Knowing our resources were stretched beyond the breaking point, I shook my head. "The only hope would be to send her to our cousin and depend on their charity to present her."

"There you go again," Victoria admonished but patted my hand to soothe the sting. "Where is your faith?"

The fiddler showed up early on the following Saturday, the second week in February. He looked older than Methuselah and had a young boy with him to carry his raggedy bedroll. Speaking with an accent that sounded French, he offered to play for his and his companion's supper and a place to sleep on the grounds. The young boy assured us in better English that his "uncle" was an excellent violinist and had played for the queen of England.

"With such a tale, they are most probably gypsies," Victoria whispered. "But it's the best opportunity we have." She was good enough not to smirk over the divine providence of their appearance. We might not have a social, but a fiddle player went a good ways past nothing toward our goal.

Before Monroe's arrival, we would have sent them away. It wouldn't have been prudent to publicize the fact to strangers that we were three women living alone. But now, with a male presence to make any scallywags think twice about doing us ill, I felt more agreeable to taking the chance.

"Monroe?" I said to claim his attention.

He shifted his intent gaze from the ragtag musician to me. "Do you dance?" I asked.

"Yes, ma'am," he answered slowly. "Not well, but passable."

I looked at the old grandpappy. "We don't have enough for a quadrille or Virginia reel, but if you play dance music, we'll barter with you."

A few hours later, after chores had been done and supper prepared, I helped Claire into one of her new dresses. She had seemed tepid about the prospect of music for the evening. So, I had not mentioned the dancing I had hoped would take place. She might abdicate the event altogether. As I helped fasten her dress, I noticed the unfinished wedding dress hanging, hidden by a worn woolen cloak. This did not strike me as a good sign.

"It won't be long before we'll be packing for Savannah," I said, as easily as one might discuss the weather.

Claire rose only partially to the bait. "I wish Mr. Tacy would get homesick so we might leave sooner."

"You know he asked us to call him Monroe. And we have more to do before we ask if he will accompany us." And we had to find more ammunition to convince him we should go, since at this point the trip would have to be financed by his charity.

Claire half turned, but I held her steady to finish her buttons. "I know, we have to make your new dresses," she said.

"We do," I concurred, then moved to the subject I wished to discuss. "And we have to finish your wedding dress. You'll be taking it with you to Savannah, I presume?"

Answered by silence, I did up the last button then patted the collar of her dress. Slowly, I took Claire by the shoulders and turned her to face me.

She looked down at my feet which were attired in the new shoes Monroe's mother had sent. "I suppose," she mumbled.

"That doesn't sound very promising."

I lifted her chin to look into her eyes. "Do you remember that the purpose of this Savannah trip was to find you a husband?" She tried to look down again but I held her firm. "Have you changed your opinion?"

"No. I mean, I don't think so —" Her eyes began filling with tears and my heart melted.

Here we had been pushing Claire at Monroe in our thoughts if not with our hands, and had had little success. In less gloomy times she would have had months, even years, to get to know her intended. I'd had six months courting from William. Of course, I had known long before his proposal that I wanted him as my husband. Claire had barely known Monroe for three weeks.

I pulled her close for a hug. "It's all right, Clarey. Knowing exactly what you want is a gift. The rest of the time each of us has to fumble for an answer." I kissed her cheek. "Don't cry. You'll know by the time we leave."

Downstairs, we met Victoria in the hallway coming in from the rear of the house, her hands occupied with empty dishes. The gypsies and Monroe had eaten out on the back porch. Monroe had said he wanted to hear any news they might bring and asked to be forgiven for deserting the dinner table. Victoria had an odd smile on her face as she passed us.

"Do you need help?" I asked.

"No," she answered, then looked at Claire. "You look very pretty tonight, sister. That new dress compliments you well."

"Thank you, sister," Claire said with a small curtsy before taking some of the dishes from Victoria.

The sound of a fiddle being tuned cut through the air. It made my heart beat faster. It had been so long, it seemed eons, since there had been music in this house. As Claire walked toward the dining room, Victoria leaned closer to me and raised her eyebrows. "Wait until you see our Monroe," she said in a theatrical whisper before following Claire.

Our Monroe.

I didn't know whether to be happy or sad about the emphasis. I would consider us fortunate to be able to claim him, but at this point, without Claire's concurrence, I couldn't see a hope or a hallelujah of accomplishing that outcome.

Earlier in the afternoon, one of our chores had been moving all the furniture back along the walls in the sitting room. I realized as I made my way into the room that we'd forgotten to roll up the rug. As I kneeled down to complete that task, Monroe stepped through the door.

To say I was surprised would be like saying Noah had experienced a rain shower. I could only stare as he came forward to help me with the rug.

"Why Monroe . . ." was all I could manage. He must have spent the better part of the afternoon preparing himself.

He'd obviously taken a bath, which given the temperature of the creek in early February could be considered life threatening. He'd also trimmed his beard and mustache, oiled and combed his hair, and looked to be wearing a new, or a freshly boiled shirt under his frock coat. He'd even tied a neckcloth.

In comparison, I felt absolutely dowdy in my second-best dress. "You're . . . beautiful," I stammered.

He flushed red from ear to ear before mumbling a "Thank you, ma'am" and set to the business of rolling the rug.

Upon entering the room a short time later, Claire awarded Monroe one initial gaping look of surprise, then refrained from turning in his direction at every opportunity. I had nearly succumbed to the rash action of shaking some sense into her when the gypsy fiddle player began to play.

The song was a classic waltz, and before I could settle onto the settee properly, Monroe stood before Victoria, offering his arm. With a regal expression, she allowed him to escort her to the center of the room and into the steps of the waltz.

Monroe turned out to be a very passable dancer, although that evening I admired his chivalry more. A man surrounded by spinster women, yet willing to entertain the lot the best he could. A duty many a soldier might shirk, more willing to face a hail of lead shot. I determined in that moment to write his mother a note and tell her how well she had raised this son. Silently, I thanked William for sending him to us.

My turn came next and I divined what Monroe had planned. He would dance with each of us by order of our birth, leaving shy and reluctant Claire for last — possibly so she would have a more difficult time refusing him. As Monroe guided me around the room I fervently hoped our sister Claire's manners had not fallen so low.

"You dance well, Monroe," I said as he led me into a turn.

"Thank you, but that would be my mother's fault. When my father determined to teach me cards at a young age, she would only allow it if I took dancing lessons."

"Well, you do her proud."

"You might not say so if I trod on your feet."

The gypsy changed the song as we reached the other end of the room again. I recognized the notes of "Come Where My

Love Lies Dreaming." William and I had danced to the same music so long ago it seemed like an entire lifetime had passed until now. My mind drifted off to familiar notes and happier days. I wished I could close my eyes, then open them to find my husband with his arms about me, guiding my steps. I would gladly dance from our sitting room into the afterworld with him without a care.

My current partner seemed to take my mood because he didn't escort me back to my seat, he continued dancing, allowing me to revel in the music and my memories for a short span of time. At the end of the last refrain, Monroe formally escorted me back to my seat before bowing. Then he approached the gypsy.

"Do you know anythin' a little more lively?" he asked.

The gypsy nodded and waited as the young boy with him took out a comb and covered it with a piece of paper. Then, as no doubt they'd done many times before, they were off into a polka. Claire gave me one wide-eyed look before she allowed Monroe to take her hand.

Suffering from inspiration, I pushed to my feet and crossed to Victoria. Better we should be embarrassed than sit like two

Spanish duennas and stare at Claire and Monroe. Laughing in a decidedly unlady-like manner, Victoria and I set off in a fe-male only, secession polka that would have set our nemesis, Mrs. Habersham, on her head if she'd witnessed it. Hopefully our sainted mother wasn't rolling in her grave.

After several more polkas, for which Claire was required to partner Monroe since Victoria and I were occupied making fools of ourselves, we all collapsed in mirth and exhaustion. Even the gypsy seemed amused at our foolishness. Successfully catching her breath, Victoria excused her-self to retrieve the pitcher of apple punch she'd left in the dining room, leaving me to fill the gap of sudden silence.

"Isn't this . . . well, stimulating?" I asked the room in general. I looked at Claire, whose cheeks were pink from exertion for the answer.

Monroe spoke instead. "Ma'am, this is better than racin' horses barebacked on the Fourth of July." Then he ducked his head slightly before glancing at Claire. "If I could manage to stay off Miss Claire's toes, that is."

Claire actually laughed, and for the first time since Monroe had arrived, I had a glimmer of hope. "He's telling tales, Julia.

I am the one who stepped on his foot."

"Only because mine was somewhere it wasn't supposed to be," Monroe countered.

As they parried with each other to take the blame, there was a sudden loud knocking at the door. Victoria, partway there already, waved to me before setting the pitcher of punch on the side table. I heard the door open. Then, as some less dignified folk might say, "all hell broke loose."

First, Victoria let out a wail to wake the snakes. I was already standing when I saw her fall backward to the floor. Monroe jumped up and grabbed the best weapon at hand, which happened to be the fireplace poker, then unsuccessfully tried to push me behind him. As I hurried past him I heard him order Claire to stay put and keep an eye on the gypsies.

I rushed to my sister's side fearing the worst, completely ignoring the men standing in the doorway. Monroe took it upon himself to address them.

"Stay right where you are or I'll put you under," Monroe threatened in a tone of voice I'd never heard him use before. He raised the poker, ready to strike, and looked like he could whip his weight in wildcats. I had no doubt he meant it, and the men must have felt the same because all seemed to stop.

I could see no blood or obvious injury on my sister so I raised her head and cradled it in my arms while patting her face. "Victoria? Please what's happened? Wake up." When I got no response, I called to Claire. "Bring a lamp." As Claire rushed to do my bidding, I raised my gaze to the man in the door.

"What have you done to her?" I demanded. Then before he could answer and as I watched, the light from the lamp shone bright enough for me to see his face.

"James? James Whitmore?"

Rather than answering my question, he asked, "What's happened to Victoria?"

"I believe she must have fainted dead away," I answered, yet I wondered why he hadn't tried to help her himself. As I loosened the button of her collar I thought to call Monroe off before he did someone damage. "Monroe, you can rest easy. I believe you've yet to meet James Whitmore. He's my sister's dead husband."

Chapter Ten

Claire, having relinquished the lamp, stepped closer to Monroe. "Are they ghosts?"

I remembered Victoria's earlier words to me, "as long as one of the ghosts doesn't knock on our door." I gazed up at James whose presence filled most of the doorway. His appearance was strange. For one matter, he wouldn't look at me or at his own wife who'd swooned at his feet. Too discomfitted to be tactful, I asked the obvious question of the obvious person. "I don't know, Claire. James, are you alive or are you spirit?"

James's face twisted with dark emotion. "I'm alive, but not better for it."

At that moment, Victoria began to revive and I shifted my attention back to her. "Vee? Come back to us, Sweet. All is well." I hoped I was telling the truth. When my sister's eyes fluttered open, she looked from my face to her husband's, and I thought she might swoon once again. But, as I knew she would, she drew herself together and tried to sit up.

"Monroe, please put down that poker and carry Victoria to the settee. Claire, pour your sister a glass of punch and run up for the salts." The fact that Victoria didn't argue when Monroe bent to lift her gave witness to the depth of the shock she'd received. I next did my best to invite the perpetrator of her shock into the house proper so we could close the front door on the cold and get to the bottom of this strange occurrence.

"James, come in. You must have been determined to get here to travel in the dark." As I watched, the man of color who had been standing behind James took his arm and guided him through the door. Then he doffed his hat as I closed the portal behind them.

"Traveling in the dark is not fearful for me, Miss Julia," James began. "You are Julia, are you not?"

"Why, yes, of course I am. I don't believe I've changed so much in two years." In my heart of hearts I knew that statement not to be true but would hold on to the conventions anyway.

"I'm sure you have not," James said.

"But I . . . I have changed a great deal. I am blind."

A small "oh" escaped me before I could control myself. The "Oh, dears" would come later. I set myself on managing this sudden crowd. We had not had so many in this house since my parents had been alive. I turned to the man who seemed to be James's escort.

"My name is Julia Lovejoy, and you would be . . . ?"

"Arliss Edwards, ma'am."

"Well, Mr. Edwards, would you escort James into the sitting room? Have either of you had supper?"

"No, ma'am."

"Go on in and try not to scare the life out of my sister again, James. We are pleased to see you alive. I'll bring in a plate for both of you."

When I turned toward the kitchen, I nearly collided with the old gypsy and his young "nephew."

"My, I'm out of breath from all the excitement," I said to no one in particular. Then I addressed the gypsy. "I don't believe we'll be having any more music tonight, but we enjoyed your concert very much. You're welcome to sleep on the grounds, and if you stop by the cookhouse on your way out in the morning, I'll leave some biscuits on the stoop."

He nodded his thanks. "I bid you good night, then."

With part of the crowd dispersed, I went out to the kitchen to raid the pie safe.

Within thirty minutes I sailed from feeling like I'd been racing at breakneck speed, to traveling at a snail's pace, as we minded our manners and waited for James and his man Arliss to finish eating. I sat next to Victoria, holding her hand for support — for her sake or mine I wasn't sure. That left Claire next to Monroe, and for once she didn't seem dismayed by the arrangement. The silence in the room, punctuated by the sound of silver scraping against plates, seemed louder than the music we'd so recently danced to. We had only cold cornbread and beans left from supper, but the men ate quickly enough to make me think they hadn't eaten at all during the day. The wait still seemed eternal. As soon as they finished, we could in good conscience ask the questions uppermost in our minds. Like how a flesh-and-blood soldier knocks on the door after he's been dead for over a year.

When the last bit of cornbread was gone, I rose to take the empty plates. Claire surprised me by moving to my side. I wasn't sure if she'd grown into another facet of her womanhood or whether she wanted to get a better look at her only living brother-in-law. As I handed the plates to her, James reached out and touched my arm.

"Tell me who is here so I may know how to make my explanations," he said in a low voice.

"Our sister Claire is here, next to me." Claire curtsied at that point then seemed to recollect he couldn't see her. She left the room quickly with a red face on the errand of dirty plates. I continued, "Then we have our friend Sergeant Tacy from Savannah who served with William. Victoria is across the room. That's all of us."

"Your parents?"

"They passed not long before we got word of your . . ." I had no idea what to say. He'd been reported missing, presumed killed, and we'd been living with that news since. I glanced at my sister who still sat in white-faced shock. *Oh, Vee.*

James closed his unseeing eyes for a moment, then opened them again. He looked older than I had remembered, older than he was in years. I wondered why he hadn't asked for Victoria, but then he knew he'd already frightened her out of her wits at

154

the front door. Since he wasn't my husband, I suppose he thought me of sterner stuff.

"Thank you, Julia," he said, before speaking to his companion. "Will you lead me to my wife?"

Arliss Edwards looked to me for direction, and I pointed to Victoria who was in the process of sitting up straighter on the settee. Pale yet resolute, she seemed frail enough to be broken by any careless move. She gathered her skirts to make room for James to sit next to her, but he didn't. Holding Arliss's arm, he approached her. Then he folded his hands in front of his belt, like a reverend or a man about to say his last words on Earth.

"Victoria? I came here to apologize for being a coward and a liar."

You can believe at this point that James had the absolute attention of everyone in the room. Claire had squeezed in behind Monroe's chair and had her hands braced on the back of it. But all eyes were on James.

"How is that, James?" Victoria asked. Her voice sounded hoarse but without quaver.

"I have allowed you to believe all this time that I was dead. When as you can see, that is not the case. After I was blinded and went missing, I intended to go on being dead to you so you might have a better life with someone else . . . someone whole." James halted for a moment, then rubbed a sleeve against his unseeing eyes. Being blind didn't seem to cure the human frailty of tears.

"But then I realized that in order for you to go on, to find another husband when I still legally lived, would make you a law-breaker and an oath breaker. I could not let that happen."

He straightened his own shoulders and for a moment I could see the soldier in him. "I've come home to divorce you."

I suddenly found myself standing again as I heard my sister say, "You'll do no such thing. Now sit down here next to me and tell me what's on your mind. I need to hear the entire story."

With Arliss's help, James slumped down onto the couch next to Victoria and rubbed his eyes again. Then he sighed. "I'm afraid I've ruined everything."

Still standing, I decided to clear the room. I moved toward Monroe and Claire. "We'll leave you two —" I said for Victoria and James's benefit, then looked directly at Arliss Edwards, "— alone."

156

"No," James said, stopping us in place. "I wish for all of you to hear what I have to say. You have a right to know, and the telling is my penance." Then he turned in Victoria's general direction and added, "That is, if you can bear it."

Victoria gazed at her husband for a long moment, then looked at me. "I can."

"Arliss already knows my story. It's hard to keep secrets from the man who sees for me," James said.

So, we sat down to hear James's tale. I must say that I wanted to know everything and felt as James did that we deserved to hear it. I did worry for Victoria, but I also knew her strength. She would not collapse from mortification, only from heartbreak. And since she'd already lived through that at the report of James's death, I figured she had it in her to hear how he came to be alive and in our sitting room.

Please God, let it not be another woman.

"I will start at the beginning of what you know. I was with the 54th at Chickamauga." His face twisted with an ironic smile. "With the artillery. Can you imagine? Me, who rarely adventured and who constantly had my nose in a book." James looked toward the room in general. "Sergeant Tacy, was it? If you served, then you know how things work in the military. It turns out I had studied more engineering than most of the men in the company. I had a talent, you see. I could sight the cannon." Out of what looked like old habit, his hand rose and patted the pocket in his vest where his spectacles still resided.

I felt a chill like a cold hand on my neck. The thought of gentle, scholarly James Whitmore with his watch fob and his glasses sighting down guns that would blow men like my own husband to bits made me want to weep. But I fought to keep my composure. I would not bring down Victoria's brave face with my own weakness.

"The intense study of angles and trajectories fit my disposition, you might say. That and the fact that I was not faced with the task of looking a man in the eye before I shot him. My regrets to all those who were brave enough, but I freely admit my lack of backbone. My targets were mostly enemy batteries, wreaking havoc on their cannon, although we were called to do battlefield work as well. On that subject, my only defense was deciding that if I became an expert at sighting I could save the lives of our men. And, I believe I did save some." He stopped and swallowed. "As for myself, I imagined I'd go deaf as a consequence of my service, since working with six or eight parrots firing at once and continuously makes a head-cracking racket. After thinking through that probability, I felt my hearing was little enough to lose in service of the great state of my birth." James appeared puzzled for a moment. "I had not considered being blinded."

Perhaps without realizing she had done so, Victoria slid her hand over James's and waited for him to continue. After a heartfelt sigh, he did.

"But my cannons were of little use at Chickamauga. The open land around the creek was rocky and broken, the rest so thick with trees you couldn't even sight a good rifle shot much less a three-inch gun. It was quite beautiful actually, and in peaceful times you might expect a red Indian to step out of the trees. If there were any Indians in the forest that day, I would hope they were smarter than the rest of us and hightailed it in a homeward direction.

"We were soldiers, and our presence was required by General Bragg. Rather than our usual battlefield array, we were ordered to move forward regiment by regiment to secure the crossings over Chickamauga Creek.

" 'They musn't have the railhead in Chattanooga,' we were told. So we — I holding a rifle instead of my artillery sight — set off to search out the Federals who were between us and Chattanooga. The first day we reached Reed's bridge, crossed and continued to advance, meeting little resistance. We were ordered to align along the creek to the north, and I imagine most of the troops accomplished that before the true battle began."

James halted his speech and drew in a breath as if the telling sapped part of the life out of him. "With some surprise, the Unionists encountered our positions and were driven back initially. We spent the night hearing the chop and crack of trees being felled to be used as breastworks.

"What I wouldn't have given for my battery of sturdy guns and a space empty of trees. We might have discouraged them from making themselves at home. By the next morning, our fate was set. We attacked but in a disorderly fashion because of the terrain. To be honest, when the fighting was at its hottest, most of our troops were lost in the trees — no battle lines, no chain of command, nothing but kill or be killed.

"And kill we did. If I had not been privy

to the sight of watching a man die at my hands before, now I had become a true veteran." James sat silent as though he couldn't go on.

"How did you come to be blinded?" Victoria asked, more in sympathy than curiosity. Knowing my sister, she was most probably doing her best to help her husband reach the end of his story so he would not have to relive the terrible emotions we could all see on his face.

"This is still a mystery to me," he answered, sadly shaking his head. "I remember the bright flash of a musket at close range, the heat of it scorching my skin, but then the world retreated.

"I awoke facedown on the musty forest floor to utter silence and plagued by a terrible thirst. I don't know if I had lain there for hours or for days. My only thought was to get to water. By habit, I searched for my spectacles and using the touch of my fingers, found them on the ground next to me. I put them on and sat up.

"The change of position fired an acute pain in the left side of my skull, and when I touched my hair, I felt the flow of new blood. Later a doctor in Ohio would pronounce that I carried a bullet in my brain, but at the time, I was ignorant to the extent of my injury. I tried to look about to see exactly where I had fallen and who of my comrades might be near, but the world seemed dim, obscured by the gray smoke of battle. I might have realized the truth then, that the battle was long over and the smoke hindering my eyes would be with me for the rest of my days, but the rest of me demanded I find water.

"My senses seemed to be returning one by one. I could hear the rush of the creek, and its music eased my soul. Using a tree within my reach, I gradually pulled myself up and set off in the proper direction, determined to get there on two limbs or four. I won't recount my journey now. There were many obstacles hindering my path besides the trees, which kept me upright, mostly the dead and dying. It is the one instance since I was blinded that I could say it is God's mercy I could not see the men I stumbled or crawled over."

I heard Claire sniff and realized my own eyes were raining tears. Victoria sat very straight, her gaze trained on her husband's unseeing eyes, and seemed determined not to cry. For him, as if her weakness might be the final straw in his composure. Monroe, his hands clasped, his forearms resting on his knees, sat motionless. He seemed to be staring at the oak planks of the floor. I wondered once again how it must be for a soldier to find a reason to live when so many had died.

James swallowed hard, as if his battle-field thirst had returned. In a calm, wifely gesture, Victoria took the cup of apple punch Claire had brought for her and pressed it into her husband's hand. He held it but didn't raise it to his lips.

"When I finally reached the creek, my only thought was to plunge my head under and drink my fill. I heard close voices, however, nothing else, not capture or eminent death mattered to me beyond water. As I splashed a handful on my face, hoping to clear my sight, one of the voices directed his words to me."

"I wouldn't drink that if I were you."

"Thinking I might see the source of the warning, I rolled slightly so I could look without turning my head and thus begin the pounding once more. The maneuver did no good. My eyesight had not cleared. I couldn't tell if he was from our side or the other. surprised myself by croaking out a reply, 'I need water.'

"You don't need water enough to drink this devil's brew."

"Not understanding his objection, since

I had waded through this very creek the day before and the water was clear and cool, my thirst overcame his advice, and I proceeded to bring my cupped hands filled with the fast moving water toward my mouth." James lowered his head. "Suddenly the owner of the voice took a double handful of the back of my coat and forcibly pulled me from the creek and up the bank several feet.

" 'What's the matter? Are you blind?' he shouted into my face. 'The water is running red with the lifeblood of this battle and the poor souls left behind.' He must have tossed a canteen at me because the weight of it hit me in the chest. 'Drink this. It'll have to do ya till the day's fightin' is done. They'll be someone along to collect you after awhile, if you're still alive.' "

Out of the corner of my eye, I saw Claire press her handkerchief over her mouth before running from the room. I thought to go after her but decided to let her think it out on her own for the moment. If she was to become a wife and mother, she must learn the harsh lessons life can teach, although the lessons of war taught to James Whitmore seemed too harsh to bear repeating. Anyone who had studied history, however, must know that mankind would make war until judgment day, for one cause or another. And soldier after kinsman would fall. I returned my attention to James and noticed he was not unaffected. He appeared to have faded with the telling.

"I heard later, that the name Chickamauga is an Indian name. It means River of Death."

A long silence ensued in which each of us seemed reluctant to move or quietly follow Claire from the room.

Victoria made the decision for all of us. She stood to her full height, no sign of the weakness she'd experienced earlier, and spoke to me. "Julia? I think we need to prepare resting places for our guests."

Hearing her call her husband a guest did not faze me. I followed her lead. "We have a parson's room around the side of the house or" — I looked to Monroe — "is there room to spare in the barn?"

Before he could answer, Victoria continued, "I thought I would put James in my room and I could share yours." She went on without waiting for dissent. "Mr. Edwards can occupy the parson's room or the barn if Monroe doesn't mind."

Monroe stood then, and I had the impression he had gotten older in the last few hours. His face seemed drawn, no sign of the grin that had convinced me he was perfect for Claire.

"There's room for one more," he said solemnly. Then after a moment of silent contemplation of my expression, he regained a modicum of his humor. He shook his head in an obviously feigned show of sadness. "We might have to evict the mule."

James, now the only one in the room left sitting, seemed unmovable. "There is more that needs telling," he announced stiffly.

Victoria rested a hand lightly on his shoulder. "We know there is, James. But this evening we've all suffered a bit of a shock at the miracle of your return and the depth of your suffering. I personally need some time to digest this surprise meal of thoughts. There will be time tomorrow to hear the rest."

I, myself, knew Victoria would sit through anything required to remove even a tiny portion of James's burden, but everyone in the room could see the effect of James's long journey and his even longer held truths. At this moment in time he needed rest, and my sister was determined he would have it.

Victoria gently removed the untouched cup of punch from her husband's hand.

"Mr. Edwards, will you help me guide my husband upstairs?"

As I watched the three of them move toward the stairs, the urge to follow left me. My sister knew how to manage her own husband without help. I had a sudden thought that the bond between us, Victoria and myself, had just been dealt a blow. A happy one, but a blow just the same. Her first, rightful attachment and duty was to her husband now, and no matter what occurred after his sudden reappearance, I would be a witness, not a participant.

Shaking off the taint of melancholy, I turned and found myself alone with Monroe.

"Claire went out the front door," he said. "Do you want me to go and find her?"

The irony of this being how we'd hoped the evening would commence, with Claire and Monroe forming a kind of bond, didn't escape me. But I knew I could not send Monroe to comfort Claire, carrying our hopes. The confession Claire had made of her fears made that impossible.

"I'll go to her," I answered and tried to smile. "The three of us have rambled every foot of this farm in dark and light. I know her favorite places to disappear so as not to be found." He nodded once at my logic. "I would appreciate you taking charge of Mr. Edwards. He was kind enough to bring James back to us, and I would have him feel welcome."

Monroe remained and watched me with some concern as he nodded once more. "I'll see to it he finds a fit place to rest. Are you all right, Mrs. Lovejoy?"

My married name surprised me, accustomed to being simply Julia for so long to my family. It reminded me of why Monroe had come to us in the first place, and the many sad stories we'd heard, stories some of us had been required to live through. Stories of the many spirits, the living and the dead, that had been broken by the bloodiest war in all of our history.

I remain, Mrs. Julia Lovejoy, had been the way I'd ended my letters to Monroe. And I had meant the intended sentiment wholeheartedly. Remaining Mrs. Lovejoy, in the present, however, seemed unproductive in the hope of mending my own spirit.

On impulse, I touched Monroe's arm. "I would ask you to call me Julia from now on, since it is the only way I can demonstrate how much I appreciate your presence and your contribution on behalf of myself and my sisters." I removed my hand from Monroe's coat sleeve and glanced up the stairs. "And now, James."

When I returned my attention to Monroe, he seemed entirely speechless, and I realized how oddly I was behaving, nearly on a level with Claire. It seemed that after our many complaints of too much work and too much solitude, the Oak Creek Plantation had been invaded after all by a hoard of strangers and family, and none of us seemed to be quite prepared.

Our devotion to Claire's wedding plot had been completely sidetracked and yet Victoria . . . Victoria had her James back, for better or for worse, and I had taken one more step toward putting my husband's memory to rest.

"I had better see to Claire," I managed before deserting Monroe altogether.

Chapter Eleven

I found my younger sister the first place I searched, in the barn with her arms clinging around old, sleepy-eyed Jeremiah's neck and her cheek pressed against his warm coat. By the lamp she must have lit to drive away the dark and hence any spirits or wandering gypsies, I could see she'd been weeping.

I ran my hand over Jeremiah's soft and stubbly muzzle before opening the stall gate and claiming my sister from his comfort.

"Clarey, Clarey, why did you run away?" I asked as I held her against my side. I knew the many good reasons I myself had wanted to escape, but I wanted to hear her own.

"I hate the war, I don't want to listen to one more word about it. *Not one more word,*" she declared with conviction.

As I rocked her, I sought through the many memories of my mother in her dealings with us for the proper words to help my motherless sister. It might have been wrong of Victoria and me to allow her to hear the tales of war and death. She'd had no real connection to the war, no interest or investment, not like Victoria and myself. Claire's perception was of some faraway conflict that had taken the comfort and joy out of our lives. Hearing the truth may have been more than she could comprehend.

"I realize in bygone days, you might have been sheltered from such harshness as you heard tonight. We all might have. But as you well know, things are different now. The war has broken over us, and the result will be with us in one form or another for the rest of our lives." Thinking of James's loss of sight, I decided we might do a better job of propping up what remained of the rest of him rather than bemoaning our own losses.

"I've lately begun treating you as an adult," I reminded her. "A woman grown and capable of marriage and of beginning a family of her own. Like it or not, you must go forward in that fashion, as I am sure you have no wish to go backward."

"I want to go to Savannah."

As if Savannah could cure her world. "You cannot escape the war in Savannah, or in any other part of this reunited country. None of us can escape."

After an extended silence filled only by the wheezing breath of the sleeping horse, she asked, "What's to become of us now?"

With a great deal of sadness, I recognized that my mother would have known exactly where to lead in any circumstance. I, on the other hand, could only place a wager on which of the many turns our lives might take. At this point of turmoil there were too many, excuse the expression, blind corners to make any sensible long-ranged choice. We must deal with the day we are given.

"Well . . . right now, I believe it is our duty to support our sister Victoria. She has received a great shock." I gave Claire a squeeze for emphasis. "Her husband has come home, not dead at all. She'll need us to follow her lead and give her the opportunity to find a footing with this new occurrence."

"How do we do that?"

"I think we do that by welcoming James into our home. By attending to his needs and his rehabilitation. He wasn't always such a melancholy man, you know."

"He wasn't? He seems like he's been sad for a hundred years."

I wanted to say it was the war which had robbed him of his good humor, but I would not revisit the subject for Claire's sake. Instead I searched for my own memories of James Whitmore as Claire had barely known him.

"He used to compose the silliest rhymes and poems for our mother, making my eyes fill with tears on many occasions — from mirth not sadness. Do you remember that at all?" She gave a slight shake of her head. "And don't tell Victoria, but I overheard him once, reciting from memory some of the most beautiful love sonnets, when he thought they were alone." I lowered my head to whisper in her ear, "I think he's read every book written by man."

"Surely not!" Claire responded, pulling back to look me in the eye. Her tears had ceased and she looked incredulous, as if I had just told a jaw-cracking lie.

I tidied her hair a bit as I answered. "Perhaps not all of them, but certainly every one he could get his hands on."

The sadness returned to her features briefly. "He'll not read any more now."

"No, he won't," I replied briskly. "But that is something you and I might consider at some future time when the shock of his arrival from the dead wears down. I imagine a man like him would be as hungry for words as any of us are for the food that sustains us. We could read to him.

"Shall we make a pact to do our best until the proper time comes for your trip to Savannah?"

Claire nodded. "I'll do my best, Julia."

I smiled at her gravity. "And I shall do my best to bring about your much awaited departure. Now come on, to bed with you. Leave Jeremiah in peace."

We walked arm in arm from the barn to the house, Claire carrying the lamp. I heard low, male voices outside our circle of light but felt no alarm. Perhaps I was growing accustomed to a crowd. At this point, finding another host of spirits taking their leisure on our front porch wouldn't have surprised me one bit. It may have even lightened my heavy heart as the only ones missing from the evening were my parents . . . and William.

As Claire and I reached the front of the house, our light illuminated Monroe and Mr. Edwards seated on the front steps seemingly waiting for us to evacuate their sleeping quarters. They both stood as we approached. I took the light from Claire, kissed her cheek, and sent her inside, since I was sure she wouldn't want to face them in her disheveled condition. With a mumbled goodnight, she ascended the steps.

"Is everything a'right?" Monroe asked after the door closed behind her.

"Yes, I'm afraid the realities of war were a little strong for her sensibilities. I believe she'll be fine."

Mr. Edwards spoke up then. "Mr. James's tale is a sad one for certain. And there's more yet to come on its heels. He's been traveling a hard road."

"And you have traveled at least part of the road along with him. Where are you from, Mr. Edwards?"

"Lately of Ohio, which is where I hooked up with Mr. James. But I have family in the next county, near the Carolina line. My daddy sent my two brothers and me North for schoolin' as free men, not runaways. When the war blew up he said we could fight, take on a trade, or do as we choose, but we could not come home until the fighten' was over."

"And the fighten' is over," I said, although feeling as though it would never end in the hearts of most who'd lived these past four years.

"Yes, ma'am," Arliss Edwards said. "Yes,

ma'am, it is. And I aim to see who of my family is left."

Having had enough war discussion for one night, or one entire week for that matter, I turned the lamp over to the care of Monroe. "I believe, after all the excitement of the evening, I shall retire. Thank you, Mr. Edwards, for delivering James back to us. We have no reward for you but our hospitality —"

"Mr. James has already paid me, ma'am," he said quickly to end my charitable speech. "And besides, you might hold on to those thank-yous. I don't believe Mr. James intends to stay on, unless his family" — he glanced in the direction of the front door and the stairs beyond — "can persuade him."

Surprised by his frank speech and feeling slighted, I asked what I had no right to ask. "And you, knowing his travails and his mind, do you think he's better off without us?" As soon as the words left me I realized how far out in uncharted waters I had sailed. Before the war, before the normal lives of my sisters and I had been turned on end, I would never have imagined trading more than ordinary pleasantries with a man of color. Our lives would have crossed no common ground. It was a testimony to the turmoil that had been brought to Oak Creek Plantation that I now stood in the dark arguing with one.

Mr. Edwards twisted the hat he held in his hands, glancing at Monroe to settle his words. Then he spoke to me. "Ma'am, I have no place to speak on his business. I do know he's been mightily knocked down and has but the last legs of his pride left to stand upright. He'll need some convincin'."

Feeling agreeable with his answer, since every woman learns early on that most men need feminine guidance at one time or another, I gave my best imitation "Victoria-on-a-mission" smile. "Then we shall have to convince him," I said with more confidence than I felt. "Now, goodnight."

Victoria was sitting at my dressing table brushing her hair when I entered the room. The glow of one candle gave enough light to see that she stared at nothing as she rhythmically pulled the bristles through her unbound hair. We'd been taught the rule of one hundred strokes, and what used to be a chore in our youth had become a welcome ritual at times. Unsure of her wish for conversation, I pulled off my wool cape and began removing my bodice as though nothing new had occurred.

After pulling a dressing gown over my petticoats, I began removing the pins from my own hair and, in the act of delivering them to their resting place, ended up directly behind Victoria at the dresser. Her gaze met mine in the mirror, and my heart seemed to swell in my breast at the unprotected emotion in her eyes. I put my arms about her shoulders and pressed my cheek to hers.

"He would not allow me to get him settled in bed," she said sadly, as though his refusal had finally cracked her shell of composure. Tears rose in her eyes. "He simply warned me to move any valuable, breakable objects out of his immediate path as he was worse than a bull in a china shop when in unfamiliar surroundings." She swallowed and halfheartedly continued to brush the ends of her hair. "I said, this is your home, James, not some unfamiliar place." She wiped at her tears with the back of one hand before taking a deep breath.

"He said all places will be unfamiliar in the dark, and he'd better get used to it. I told him I refused to leave him sitting on the side of the bed like a stranger and forced him to allow me to remove his boots. But that was the extent of his patience." She looked down at the brush in her hands. "He said if I had any feelings for him whatsoever, that I would please leave him alone."

I hugged her hard and closed my eyes. As was the usual case with me, words of wisdom seemed as remote as the long-dead dialogue of forgotten kings. I said the only thing which came to mind. "Mr. Edwards has told me James has suffered a great blow to his pride, and that we will have to convince him of our intent to keep him here."

"But how could James say, if I had any feelings for him? He knows I —"

"Yes, he knows." I rocked her a bit, like I suspected a mother might to comfort a child. "But he has been so long with strangers and so long in his private darkness he needs to be reminded."

Victoria remained quiet, though I could feel a new rush of warm moisture against our pressed cheeks. I opened my eyes to gaze at my sister in the mirror once more.

"I have another plan for us to take up," I said, shooting in the dark as I was wont to do. "And I've already enlisted our Claire."

"What plan is that?" Victoria asked, sounding more like herself — suspicious.

"We have it that we shall rehabilitate James the best we know how. We shall feed him good food, read to him his favorite books or something new if we can beg, borrow, or steal it. And you shall convince him our lives would be one continuing tragedy if he were to leave us again.

"You do wish for him to stay, don't you?" I asked, without fear of the answer. I merely needed to hear her say it out loud.

"Yes, I wish him to stay." Her eyes teared once more. "With all my heart."

After a brief, parting hug, I loosed her and straightened, hoping to appear businesslike even though teary-eyed, half undressed, and beginning to shiver with the cold. As was the normal case for me, I had found out all I needed to know before taking action. My sister wished her husband to stay, and stay he would. We would see to it. "We'll have to put aside our wedding dress plan for the moment and attend to our new challenge."

"I'm sorry. I had forgotten about Claire and Monroe," Victoria said rather guiltily. "Did anything hopeful occur after I left?"

"Well, no," I answered, taking the brush from her idle hand and starting on my own hair. "Claire fled to the barn and awarded Jeremiah her heartfelt attentions rather than face her destiny. But all is not lost." I smiled into the glass. "She still wants to go to Savannah."

I threw off my dressing gown, kicked away my falling petticoats, and climbed into the bed under the quilts taking the brush with me. "Blow out the candle and come to bed. We've done enough for today."

As she complied with my request, I made room in the bed for her and hugged her close, spoon-style for warmth, like we used to do as children. "Everything will seem different by the light of day," I mumbled. But then I remembered that the light of day would mean little to James and the set of his mind. We'd have to provide him with other kinds of enlightenment.

"Did you see Monroe's face when James spoke of the battle?" Victoria asked in the dark.

"No," I confessed. "When I spared a glance, he'd been staring at the floor."

"We have done a terrible thing, all of us, by supporting, even championing, such death and destruction."

Yes, most probably we had, I thought, but to save judgment until after the fact would not be realistic or charitable to those in the vanguard. No matter what terrible weight we had brought down on our own heads with our good intentions, the deed was long done.

"We in the South have broken our own hearts, Vee, sending off the best of us to be cut down in the fields and forests. How could we have known? Even Abraham Lincoln's God cannot punish us further." Thinking of my ever-practical and independent father, I wondered if Abraham Lincoln's government, left to wield the weighty matter of reuniting the Union without his guidance, might accomplish what the war had not — the total destruction of the South. I could only hope that, as with the fighting, the Reconstructors would somehow pass us by. Otherwise our future, or lack of such, might be too much to bear.

Remembering our mother's talent for living the Tuesday of each Tuesday, and the Wednesday of all the Wednesdays we might ever have, and not cringing before an uncertain future, I added, "As our mother would have said, we will do our best to heal our wounds and go on. I believe we will begin with James."

Victoria squeezed my hand. "We will," she said. And it sounded like a promise.

The morning brought hungry men to the

kitchen as dawn was breaking through the trees. Not the least of which were the two gypsies who had played so happily for us the evening before. The night had gone colder and a heavy white frost covered the ground, merely the sight of it making one shiver harder. The old man and the boy were in a rush to get on their way, standing in the cold, shuffling foot to foot, hoping no doubt to find a less crowded and possibly more prosperous crossroads before dark.

I sent the gypsies off with the promised biscuits and a lump of precious butter to share between them as Claire and Vee broke eggs and carved some bacon to prepare breakfast for the rest of our guests.

I returned to the warmth of the kitchen in time to watch Monroe, who had assumed the role of temporary member of the family, pour coffee for himself, Mr. Edwards, and a cup to be delivered to James before settling himself on the stool situated in the corner of the kitchen nearest the stove. When Mr. Edwards picked up the coffee and made his way into the house bound for James's room, Victoria's gaze followed him with what looked like unspoken requests on the tip of her tongue. She didn't speak out loud, however, and as soon as Mr. Edwards cleared the door, she went back to her work with the second batch of cornmeal for flapjacks.

By the time we'd transported breakfast to the dining room, Mr. Edwards and James were making their way down the stairs, Mr. Edwards counting each step as they went. Victoria pulled out a chair at the head of the table for James and then moved to her own place at his right. We had set the place on the left for Mr. Edwards, since James might require his assistance, and next to him, Monroe. But as the rest of us filled out the seating, Mr. Edwards stood uncertainly behind the chair meant for him and gave me a questioning look.

In our county only the richest families with large tracts of land had been slaveholders, and in these times when all traditions had been upended, I had no idea what the proper course might be. I didn't know if we should object to Mr. Edwards's presence at our table, or if he would feel disinclined to dine with us, but, with my mother's practicality and civility running in my blood, I believed it best to include him lest I be a disappointment to my family and myself. After all, as I had told Monroe, this man had been a friend to our James and I wanted him to feel welcome. Our table, such as it was, would have to do.

Without further information, I simply followed my usual course and fumbled forth. "Will you have molasses on your flapjacks, Mr. Edwards?" I asked, holding out the pot to him.

"Yes, ma'am," he said then sat down without further ado and the meal commenced.

I asked Claire to say grace, and she complied with a bowed head and the traditional, "Thank you Lord for this food we are about to receive . . ." adding one inspired new touch at the end of the verse. "And thank you Lord for the safe return of our brother, James. Amen." Simple, yet a good beginning.

Then, quiet reigned. Those of us, the men, whose minds seemed to be solely on filling their bellies, were content to spend their attentions on knives and forks. After mapping out the territory of his place setting with gentle touches, James did an admirable job of finding the food on his plate with only occasional direction from Mr. Edwards.

Victoria, to his right, spent very little time eating, using the opportunity to study her husband without his knowledge. Her expression remained sad and serious but not without hope. Monroe, as I mentioned, could flatter any cook, no matter the talent, with the way he put away food. The thought crossed my mind to warn him, lest he grow as round as Reverend Pembroke, but I let it go. I had no business tinkering with Monroe's appetite.

If any at the table might have been concerned whether the manners of free men of color might be foreign to our own, that concern was handily put to rest by Mr. Edwards himself. Other than asking to use his plain crockery coffee cup rather than my mother's china cup resting in its saucer, he made do with the rest of us.

When we'd eaten our fill, or reached the bottom of the dish, whichever came first, I knew it was time for someone to begin the conversation. If we were to pursue any of our various plans or even retain common courtesy, we would have to talk to one another with more variation than, "Please pass the bacon or the salt."

"I thought, since this is Sunday, that James and Mr. Edwards might make use of it for a well-deserved rest while the rest of us attend church."

Forks stopped midair for several heartbeats, then half the table spoke simultaneously.

"But I thought —" Victoria began.

"Can't we miss church today?" Claire asked, ever willing to be spared another sermon.

"The gypsy told me he heard some wild turkeys over to the west —" Monroe contributed.

"I have business to conclude with Victoria today," James said last, sobering the group.

Victoria gazed at me with a rare helpless expression on her face. Neither of us had missed the word, "conclude."

"James, you cannot appear after two years, walking from heaven knows where to arrive here, and then disappear after one day. We require more of your company than that," I said.

"But I told you why I've come back. There is no need, and it would be unkind to delay any longer than necessary," James replied.

In what I knew to be a search for control, Victoria raised her napkin to her lips before lowering it and twisting it in her hands. The room returned to silence.

Mr. Edwards cleared his throat. "Mr. James, remember when I told you I stepped on that stob crossing the creek the other day?"

James nodded.

"Well, my foot, it's fairly swelled and it could sure use a day without walkin'."

James remained silent and frowning.

"Is there some pressing business you have to attend? We'll be happy to send a letter explaining your delay," I offered, hoping to tip the scales.

"I suppose one more day won't be a hardship, that is . . ." He shifted his unseeing regard in Victoria's general direction. "If it isn't an imposition for you, Victoria."

"I will be happy to have you for one more day," Victoria said in a low voice.

"Then it's settled," I announced before any minds could be changed. "Now about church . . ."

"Could I please be excused from church? I need to practice my reading. Remember I promised I would read to the rest of you from the magazine Mr. — I mean Monroe's mother sent and I —" With all eyes on her, Claire's face went the color of beets. "I'm out of practice," she managed.

We should never doubt that others are paying attention, I reprimanded myself. Claire was doing her part, sooner than expected, but more welcome because of her own ingenuity. She could further our plans and escape church in the same deft stroke.

"I think you're right, Claire. Don't you agree, Victoria?" My older sister concurred with a stately nod. "Although I believe some of your practice should be taken with mother's bible. That way you won't sink into the heathen ways Reverend Pembroke claims are in abundance these days."

"I will, Julia," she said, looking contrite.

I knew it was a hoax but couldn't fault her. She had run the gauntlet and obtained the prize.

With everything seemingly settled, the men excused themselves giving the three of us, Claire, Victoria, and me, more time to ourselves to conspire.

Half an hour later, as I tossed out the used bucket of wash water from the breakfast dishes, I found Monroe and Mr. Edwards deep in conversation near the back door. Both were wearing their heavy coats and Monroe was carrying his rifle.

"I thought I'd go see if I can spot one or two of those turkeys, Mrs. Love — I mean Julia," Monroe said, answering my unspoken nosiness and obviously doing his best to honor my request concerning my name.

I put the empty bucket on the steps and walked over to them.

"Arliss and I might check on that second buck I saw the other day, as well. We've got more mouths to feed, and if the fates are willing, we might even come up with enough bounty for a little homecoming feast in honor of Mr. James."

Being practical to the bone and not a little bossy, I pointedly studied Mr. Edwards's feet. They looked sturdy enough but . . . "I thought you needed to rest your foot," I said. "Hunting doesn't seem like rest to me."

"My foot is fit, ma'am." He smiled in a conspiratorial way. "If Mr. James asks for me, you could say I'm in the barn asleep, or resting."

In that moment, I was never so happy to have followed my instincts. Mr. Edwards had lied about his foot to help us. To give us time to do a little "convincin' " as he'd called it. He would be welcome at my table from now into the future.

"Thank you, Mr. Edwards, on behalf of all of us."

He looked down, but I could see he was pleased. "Mr. James should be with a family who loves him, ma'am. I can see that y'all do. I'll help what I can."

"Since you're so good with Mr. James," Monroe injected, a slight smile lightening the moment. "Do you have any secret, mystical powers to use on a thickheaded mule?"

I laughed, because I knew the mule in question.

Mr. Edwards looked puzzled but answered in a helpful manner. "Well, my daddy used to say you had to talk to 'em. Tell 'em how fine they are and how much money you paid for 'em. Make 'em want to show off."

Monroe shook his head ruefully. "Well I've talked to this one, but the words I've used ain't fit for his ears or anyone else's. You want to give him a go?"

Mr. Edwards nodded.

Turning toward the barn, Monroe winked at me and continued speaking to Arliss. "If you have no more success than I did, we'll just drag him out back, shoot him, and cook him. You know I ate some mule when I was in the army and it whaddn't half bad."

I returned to the house unaccountably lighter at heart. If the main of us were in league to keep James on Oak Creek Plantation, then how could we fail? I stopped before stepping through the back door and raised my gaze to the clear blue of the heavens. *Thank you God, for James's return and for Arliss Edwards. And, thank you William, for Monroe.*

Chapter Twelve

Left alone with James, we — my sisters and I — were like three wary cats with a newcomer in our midst. We circled and huddled and whispered our options while James waited patiently for us to declare ourselves. He finally put his figurative foot down, requesting our presence in the sitting room and holding out an arm for one of us to guide him. Victoria claimed the duty. Claire and I followed, and though I wasn't sure of her feelings, mine were in a firm knot of trepidation. Our opportunity to "convince" was upon us, and we had not come up with a solid course of action.

"Victoria? I have more to tell you and it cannot wait," James began.

"If you feel it's necessary," Victoria replied, folding her nervous hands around a handkerchief held at the ready.

James seemed surprised by this. "Don't you want to know where I have been so long? Why you haven't received any word from me since my fateful last battle?"

I watched Victoria choose her words and held my breath. "Of course I want to know whatever you wish to tell me," she said. "But, if you mean, do I demand an accounting, then no. I am content that you are here, safe and sound."

A reply sputtered, but words appeared to fail James.

Victoria glanced at me briefly, shifted her shoulders to an attitude of readiness for anything then said, "I suppose I do need to know the why of your plan to divorce me and leave Oak Creek."

"I told you," James began as a cornered man might face patience when he'd expected hysterics. "I want you to be free to have a new life. You deserve better than to be chained to my destiny as a blind man."

"Is that the whole of it?" Victoria asked. She seemed as calm and collected as any barrister gathering testimony from a witness, but I knew her heart. I knew what James had forgotten. Victoria might present a calm and logical demeanor, but her emotions ran deep, especially loyalty to the ones she loved. I'd been lucky enough to be a recipient of the aforementioned loyalty and would testify to its potency.

"I've mentioned there is much more —"

James answered. "I was in the Camp Chase, Ohio, prison for months, then released because I was no further threat as a soldier."

Claire fidgeted next to me, expecting more gruesome tales I supposed, but before I could reassure her, Victoria stopped him. "We have years ahead of us for you to tell me all, James. What I want to know, and expect to hear in the next words you speak, is whether this divorce business only involves your injury and the noble decision for me to go on."

"Why, yes of course. I'm worthless to anyone, and another mouth to feed. Why should you be burdened with my failings?"

"This is not about another woman? Another life you wish to pursue?" My sister persisted. "Because if it is, I would rather know the truth of my ruination than be spared by noble lies."

James actually chuckled before shaking his head, in disbelief I surmised. "And you imagine I am so charismatic as to receive the attentions of other women? A blind man who has lived on the charity of southern sympathizers, whose only aim in life is to let the others around him find a better path?"

"I don't have to imagine in the least."

Victoria sniffed as if insulted. "I know your many good qualities and expect that others must see them as well. I married you, after all, and not without admiration . . . and love."

James hung his head as if he'd experienced another wound. This one closer to his heart than the one he'd received to his head. "How can I convince you this is the best way? You have no idea how difficult it is to deal with the world without sight. How could I remain in our marriage and force you to find ways to feed us through charity from your family or friends?" He raised his regard as though he could see her face. "I am left with nothing but memories of the life I had envisioned, and a small pension from our new government."

"And me," Victoria added in a solemn but stubborn tone. "Us," she added, lifting a hand toward the sisters James couldn't see.

"I don't know, you can't possibly —" he began.

"Where are you headed in pursuit of pressing business if you have no future planned?" Victoria commenced, holding on to her advantage.

"I have no destination except to return to the South," James confessed. "I thought to go as far as Arliss might take me, perhaps to North Carolina. After that, there is a void of expectation."

"Then stay here with us."

"Victoria, please. Don't make a hasty decision you will regret in a month or a year. I would rather be dead and buried than make you miserable."

"Why is that, James?"

"I — because I care for you and your future."

"Care for me, as a friend, as a sister . . . or as a memory?"

James swallowed, perhaps again experiencing the dry heat of battle — emotional battle in this case. "I care for you —" He stumbled. Surrender loomed, even a soldier without sight could recognize it. "I love you as a wife. I always have, always will," he admitted with a sigh. "I'll do whatever it takes to ensure your happiness."

Victoria drew in a long, deep breath and blinked to reinforce her control. "Then we are in agreement on that much at least. Now, I would ask a boon from you, as your wife. I would ask you to remain here, on Oak Creek with us until I can make this informed decision you seem to think I need. If there is no pressing reason for you to journey on, then I don't consider it too much to ask."

Silence fell. Claire fidgeted once more which should have warned me, but I, too, felt caught in the drama. I didn't react until too late.

"If you decide to leave, then you could travel with us to Savannah when we go," Claire added helpfully.

I suppose Claire had taken me seriously when I'd explained to her about facing adulthood. She'd assumed she could give an opinion since she'd matured to the point of having one.

Both James and Victoria looked in our direction. I could almost feel Claire shrinking by my side and didn't know whether to drag her from the room for giving James another chance to disagree, or just clap a hand over her mouth and return the course of the conversation back over to Victoria.

Victoria took the matter out of my hands. She smiled at Claire, which worried me even more. "That will be our agreement then," Victoria said. "We intend to travel to Savannah next month." She didn't even glance in my direction. "The week before we leave, you and I will decide if you'll be returning to Oak Creek with us. Is that fair and equitable?"

"Oh yes, to me," James agreed, sounding

miserable. "But as for the rest of you, I'm not so sure."

"Then it's settled," Victoria concluded.

Now I know you may be thinking that I took Claire out to the barn immediately after this for, instead of a spanking as a child might require, a decent thrashing fitting of her advanced age. Her one-purpose course continued to rub on my good humor. But then she did something completely exceptional, and I marveled again at her burgeoning instincts.

"Would you mind if I read from the bible now, Julia, as you mentioned at breakfast? I want to improve my reading aloud before we make the trip so I can impress our city cousins with my country education."

Claire was not only growing up, she was growing quite skillful in the womanly art of making a plan and sticking to it.

"That would be very nice," I said.

"James, would you mind? I'm not very good at reading with an audience, but I so want to improve."

James, in the least stunned by the previous exchange with his wife and at the most worn out from his attempt to fall on his philosophical sword to save the family, nodded and managed a weak but encouraging smile. "Of course dear. It's been awhile since I've been to services. Perhaps hearing the words will suffice to save my soul."

Before Claire could rise to retrieve our mother's bible, I pulled her to me and kissed her cheek soundly. I realized then that between the three of us, James Whitmore had not a ghost of a chance at freedom unless he could find my father's pistol to keep us at bay.

As though Savannah may have become our fate, a letter from our cousins addressed to Victoria arrived three days later. In that time the new and old occupants of Oak Creek had at least retained a spirit of cooperation even if they had not grown accustomed to each other and the changed circumstances they were experiencing.

The weather, fickle as ever in February, had gone temperate, giving us a slight respite from diligent efforts at staying warm. So much so, that Victoria and I set out to boil the laundry and hang it to dry before the next icy blast would prevent us from doing so. Claire had been assigned to pump fresh water and haul firewood with help from Monroe and Mr. Edwards, while Victoria and I labored with lye soap and washboards, piles of bed linens and soiled clothes.

The boy delivering the letter found us in the backyard with sleeves pushed up, and bending over boiling pots of wash water. The boy's arrival reminded me of the day we'd received the first letter from Monroe, and my gaze shifted to him momentarily as he hefted the ax to split more kindling. My sisters and I had been so different then, a mere two months ago, living like three fading ghosts in the big, empty house of our youth.

In the middle of my musing, Monroe's eyes met mine briefly, and I turned my attention back to what I was about to do before I made a slip and scalded us all. But my mind remained on the varied events of the recent past. Everything had changed since the final night of October when we'd put our hands on our mother's sewing shears and pledged to make a wedding dress while praying for a husband, a future for Claire. It was a humbling thought, how quickly the world could work when the spirits were willing.

Our only failure had been in directing the changes. Although, I suspected, when one asked God for His favor in an enterprise, it was rather impertinent to think one should then be required to direct His favor in any chosen way. We had received more than we'd bargained for and no clear indication of how to portion out our bounty.

I remained committed to our scheme of Monroe for Claire even in the face of the current confusion of James's return although we seemed no closer to that goal, no matter how much meddling and maneuvering we applied. And now this letter from Savannah . . . was that to be Claire's salvation?

Looking somewhat wilted from our current steaming occupation, Victoria dried her hands on her apron and took the letter, opening it with a flourish while Claire traveled to the kitchen to find the delivery boy a small treat for his ride back to town.

"My dearest Victoria," she read aloud when Claire had returned.

We were all pleased and relieved to have word from you after the preceding unpleasantness. As no doubt you have heard, we have suffered under military occupation, and although we weren't forced out of our homes by General Sherman, as occurred in Atlanta, we were securely under the Federal's watchful eye for this past year. Ru-

mors are always afloat, and I am sick to death of it. I can only hope for brighter days henceforth and that providence will soon favor restoration of our former circumstances.

Mr. Langhorn bids you and your sisters good wishes. Heavens, so much has happened since we lost our aunt — your lovely mother, Amelia. Sarah and Luly each have an addition to their families as Nathan was paroled after nearly succumbing to typhus, and Steven remained in Savannah during the war serving in the home guard. Our firstborn, Frank, and his family remain in Europe where they traveled before the fateful firing on Fort Sumpter. Thank goodness for that. Their good management of the Langhorn business interests, translated far from the war and the Union, have served the family well. We hope to visit them in the coming year.

I can only imagine the discomfort and fear you girls have had to face out there in the country alone. My husband told your mother many times that city life would better suit her. Now, you are left with the results of her choices. We of course would be happy to see you in our fine city at some projected date. In the foreseeable future, *however, our house on Adams Street is filled to overflowing. If you are determined, I'm reasonably sure we can find some accommodation, if not with us, then with some of our good friends. We all have our own inconveniences to overcome. Please write with your plans when they are settled.*

Yours faithfully,
Cousin Lydia

Victoria was frowning as she folded the letter and handed it to Claire. "I hardly detect a wealth of welcome," she commented before bending back to her task of stirring the wash water. "Certainly no offer of help."

I nodded in agreement, trying not to jump to judgment as I might have done in the past. "We have no idea what their true circumstances are, since it seems both their daughters and their families have come home to roost." Then I recalled a line from the letter. "I would think planning a trip abroad would be difficult for them, however."

Victoria sent me a sideways smile. "Do you suppose it's as difficult as our planning a trip to Savannah?"

In the grand scheme of things, we could

walk to Savannah if we had to. There could be no walking to London though, someone would have to pay the passage in Union greenbacks or gold. With some effort I reined in my disappointment. Our cousins, after all, had never been close. Even before the war, the contact with them had been barely sufficient for us to claim them as family. Our mother had done most of the work of keeping in touch, since Frank Langhorn had been her only living sibling. His wife Lydia on the other hand had felt no such responsibility.

In the light of our cousin's indifference, the generosity of Monroe's mother to three women she'd never met seemed somewhat saintly. It made it increasingly difficult for me to think of asking Monroe for yet more as we had planned. If only Claire would take an interest in him, beyond a means to an end. If only —

"When should we write that we are coming?" Claire asked. She held the letter as though it contained an engraved invitation and a fully paid train ticket. It seemed the veiled reference to a full house had passed her by.

I returned to my scrubbing, waiting for Victoria's wisdom on the subject. She didn't fail me.

"Later, after supper, we'll sit down with a calendar and decide. But —" she held Claire's happy gaze, "— we shall not announce it to the men until we are ready. We still have dresses to sew. Your wedding dress in particular has been neglected lately."

Claire's excitement fled at the mention of a wedding. She slipped the letter into the pocket of her apron and nodded.

"Now here." Victoria picked up a heavy basket of clean linens and transferred it to Claire's hands. "Hang these out while we finish the rest."

As Claire moved out of earshot, Victoria tugged my arm to get my attention. "I've had a revelation," she said.

I waited.

"I have suddenly realized why our original plan for Claire and Monroe has foundered. We haven't finished the dress." She stared at me, willing me to understand. "How can we commit our hearts to something and not finish it, then still feel it can succeed?"

She was right. The revelation struck me with equal power. We had been swayed from our purpose by the surprise of all we'd somehow set in motion. Now was not the time to leave the symbol of our hopes hanging in the back of Claire's closet undone. We had to reinvest our efforts, gather our faith, and complete what we'd started.

"Sister," I said. "I do believe you've hit the nail on the head." I turned to watch Claire fling a wet bedsheet over the line, then angled my head toward the laundry that would take up the rest of the day and part of the morrow. "First we make a clean start, then we'll set upon the dress with new enthusiasm."

"We must have Claire's help," Victoria said gravely. "Without her the wedding plan may come to naught since she's the one to wear it."

"We'll have it," I assured her with not a thought in my head of how to make that happen. But then, we'd begun the entire enterprise with little more than a wish. Making a long-range plan might spoil the whole affair.

After a busy day of harder than normal labor, my shoulders and back felt ill-used. My feet, however, were more restless than usual. It might have been the short spell of warmer weather, which whispered of spring, or it might have been the lack of time to come to grips with the sudden change of our daily routines but, after supper, I found myself wanting a walk.

As had become the habit since James's return, Claire would retire to the sitting room and read aloud to him along with anyone else who wished to listen for an hour or so. Tonight her audience would consist of merely Victoria and James, since I was not in the humor to sit still.

I left the house with only a light shawl against the cooler night air and headed down the front drive. The sun had already dropped behind the trees but still shed streaks of pink and purple light into the clouds. All in all it was a beautiful evening, the more precious since winter remained with us while the memory of summer sailed the horizon, as distant as the first stars of the twilight.

It had been so long since I'd had a stretch of time alone that my head seemed to ring with the voices of others, and my thoughts were hopelessly intertwined with the various plans and hopes for my sisters. Even my sleep was crowded since Victoria still shared my bed. I had not dreamed in weeks, or if I had, there had been no room in my mind for the memory of it.

I drew in a deep calming breath. The air around me was still and quiet, except for the calls of a few winter birds moving through the forests. I was as alone as I would likely be for awhile, and my thoughts turned to my own future.

Thinking of *my* future was an unfamiliar venue for me. In the last few years I had been much more accustomed to thinking of past, happy memories, to get through the day, to ward off the dreams of grief. But something had changed since James's arrival. I'd realized that Victoria now had a future. Her husband had returned from the dead and for better or for worse, they would see life through together. And Claire . . . we were doing our best to help her find happiness. I still had high hopes of marrying her off to Monroe.

That left *me*.

I pulled my shawl closer around my shoulders and tried to imagine what I would do with the rest of my days. Oh, I would always make myself useful. Victoria would need all the help she could get to provide for herself and James. We might even have to sell Oak Creek if things went downhill any further. A dismal prospect. I looked toward the road which ran east to west, from the place of my birth onward to the remainder of the world and kept walking. By the time I reached the stacked rail fence several minutes later, the sky had gone crimson and indigo like the maligned flag of the Confederacy and the victorious banner of the Union. All of us would live under the same sky, the same government from now on. At least the killing was done.

But that didn't solve my present dilemma. How should I go on? Catching myself slipping into the past but not knowing where else to turn, I allowed one last effort.

"What am I to do, William?" I asked the growing dusk. "I truly miss you but I have to find some other purpose to my life besides grief. Now that James is back . . . what of me?"

I leaned on the high rail of the fence with my chin on my crossed arms and sighed. I waited. But, as in the past, only the settling quiet of the night answered my question. A chattering bird making a noisy entrance to his nightly roost caught my attention. I watched as he greeted and then rearranged the other birds who had arrived before him on the low branches of a spruce tree.

The sky was purple now, nearing full dark. The thought crossed my mind that I should go back, but I remained a little while longer. I had set out to settle my mind and had barely begun the process.

Then suddenly, I realized I wasn't alone

at the fence. Out of the corner of my eye I saw a telltale brightness and a slight movement. Slowly, so as not to startle myself or the sight before me, I turned my head to the right, toward our front gate.

I thought I would have been more used to seeing them by this time, but the first vision of him sent a thrill of unnatural power through me. There is something electrical in glory. For a shining moment, I thought my William had finally come home to answer my heart's painful questions.

But the man at the gate wasn't William. It — He was an officer. I could see that by his blouse and jacket. He rested against the outside rails of the fence, smoking a carved pipe and watching the night, much as I had been doing myself. Although being a soldier, the war obviously still on his mind, a rifle stood propped against the fence beside him.

In the darkness, his form seemed to flicker with an inner light, as though daylight waited on the other side of his shoulder. He paid no heed to me. He plainly waited and watched, for what or whom I could not guess. After several moments, he uncrossed his arms and turned his head slightly in my direction. As our eyes met, he slowly flickered once then faded from view as one might extinguish a candlelight into rising smoke.

My heart pounded several strident times in my chest, and I had the sudden urge to cry. Not from fear, but from the frustration of not knowing what it all meant. I had received a sign and felt as blind as James when it came to deciphering it.

Footsteps behind me ended my deliberations. True fear seized me then, and I spun toward the source expecting to face more ghosts, only to find Monroe following the road toward me.

I raised a hand to my heart to try to ease its frantic beat and gulped in more night air as he approached.

"Are you well, Julia?" Monroe asked, looking concerned.

"Yes," I replied with a rush of shaky breath. "You startled me, is all."

"I'm sorry. I didn't know I was sneaking up on you. I just thought to stretch my legs."

I nodded in acknowledgment and took my time getting over my fright as he advanced to stand at the fence on my left. We leaned together then and watched the road, very like the day Victoria and I had stood in the same spot and witnessed the company of ghost soldiers marching along in the snow. Because of the growing darkness and my current skittishness, I decided against bringing up the apparition I'd just witnessed. Perhaps the specter might even return for Monroe to see, and then we could discuss it. In lieu of that improbability, I chose another subject.

"You and Mr. Edwards have done well hunting. I can't remember the last time this house has experienced such a bounty of meat."

Monroe chuckled. "Well, yes . . . we've done well. But I think Arliss is more interested in hunting wood than deer."

"What do you mean?"

Monroe pulled a pipe from his jacket pocket along with a pouch of tobacco. "He seems to have begun a romance with your trees," he said, then asked, "Do you mind if I smoke?"

My mind skipped back to the ghostly officer with his carved pipe as I answered, "No, go right ahead. Now, what is this about trees?"

"It's his trade, he fashions furniture from certain woods. He seems to have found the promised land on Oak Creek. I tell you, we couldn't walk half a mile without him stopping to admire an ash or a walnut tree with the attentions of the lovesick.

"And when we built the fire in the smoker for the meat, he insisted on finding some hickory and cherry wood to add, saying he was sure we hadn't tasted anything so fine."

"It sounds as though Mr. Edwards has a talent."

"That he does," Monroe agreed as he lit his pipe. "I don't know how good he is at building furniture, but he can get that low-born son-of-a-mule to do almost anything. I've never seen the like. Now you and I both know the disposition of that mule is, well . . . reluctant."

His choice of words, a ringing under-statement if I had ever heard one, brought a smile to my mouth. As the glow of the pipe reflected in his eyes I could see he was enjoying the moment.

"Well, when Arliss gets to talking to him, telling him how handsome he is and how strong, that mule practically stands up and dances to any tune Arliss chooses. He's even given him a name, calls him Samson. I've a good mind to let him take him when he leaves. I'm tired of fightin' with that four-legged train wreck and can't bring myself to tell him he's pretty. Not after what he did to my foot."

The mention of Mr. Edwards leaving

brought back my apprehensions for the future full force. "Has Mr. Edwards mentioned when he might go?" I asked, doing my utmost to sound unconcerned.

Monroe surveyed the road in the darkness as he took another puff on his pipe. "He and Mr. James spoke about it, but I wasn't enlightened as to the decision. I do think Arliss is wantin' to get on to his family home since he's so close."

"And James is reluctant to let him leave . . ." I said, thinking out loud. Victoria and James were still very careful around one another, although she spent more time in her own room in the evenings, helping him prepare for sleep. I had heard their voices as I passed in the hallway, but during the day James remained distant.

"It's a hard thing for a man to be blind, to be half of what he was before," Monroe said. "I'm not sure I could have accepted it as much as he has."

I thought of William and how I would have loved him still, blind or not, if only he'd come back. "Men think differently than women about such things, as I'm sure you know. We tend to work together to deal with whatever comes our way and do the best we can."

"And a man would rather die honorably

on the field face to face with his destiny than lose his future," he said to the night. "It's a hard thing, that's all, especially for the ones left behind."

"I would have been elated to see William in any condition, but you are right, he would not have been happy. Poor James."

The cold, winter stars were out in force now as we fell to silence on such a sad note. The feather of a breeze touched the back of my neck and made me shiver. I pulled my shawl higher.

"I saw another of our ghostly walkers out here tonight," I confessed.

Monroe turned to discern my face in the fading light. He didn't look alarmed, only interested. "What kind of walker was that?"

"He wasn't walking precisely," I corrected myself. "He was leaning along the fence, just there by the front gate, smoking a pipe . . ." I added lamely, since Monroe had his own pipe clamped firmly between his teeth. "An officer with a rifle beside him. He seemed to be watching, as though waiting for something. Why do you suppose they've made Oak Creek a gathering place? There were no battles to speak of within fifty miles of here."

Taking his pipe from his mouth, Monroe turned toward the road again and propped one booted foot on the bottom rail. The smell of tobacco smoke drifted around me as he looked up the road and down, then slowly turned to contemplate the lights of the house in the growing gloom. Finally, reaching a conclusion, he answered, "Perhaps it's your husband's doing, ma'am. Maybe he's asked them to look out for this place, for you and your sisters, until you get through this trial of war and reconstruction." He faced me then. "I know if I were on the other side, I would send whomever I could."

My heart pounded with several excited beats. I felt as though he had gifted me with *the answer*. To what, I wasn't sure. I only knew the weight of the future I had so recently carried down the drive on my tired shoulders had left me. Tears of joy and relief rose in my eyes and without considering, I hugged Monroe. "Thank you," I managed. "Thank you, so very much."

Monroe seemed more confused than properly thanked, but my heart was too full to explain. I looked up at the diamondlike stars above our heads, and even though they blurred in my teary vision, they were still beautiful. I opened my arms, my heart, and spoke to the sky. "Thank you, William."

Chapter Thirteen

As Victoria and I prepared breakfast early the next morning, Monroe sat as usual in the corner by the stove drinking coffee. Having relegated him to the barn with few comforts, I saw no reason to deprive him of the one he'd found for himself. We'd grown accustomed to working around him, and after his kind words of the evening before, I felt his presence comforting.

I had just finished carving some bits of ham when Victoria peered into the flour barrel. "We'll have to make a trip down to Tate's soon. We're almost out of flour."

"The coffee is low as well. Perhaps day after tomorrow," I answered. "I'll take Jeremiah into Stoneman." We both knew we had another day of pressing and folding laundry before we could proceed to anything more time consuming. And then there was the wedding dress. . . .

At that moment, with the unfinished dress and Claire in my thoughts, I heard her outside, shouting our names. "Julia, Victoria!" Before I could wipe my hands and open the kitchen door, she barged inside nearly hysterical.

"It's Jeremiah! He's down in his stall." She threw her arms around me and held on. "He's sick." But before I could answer or question her further, she spied Monroe and immediately loosed me to go to him. "Please," she begged, taking his hand. "Please come and help him."

Monroe stood at her insistence. "He seemed like himself when I passed his stall earlier," he said, putting down his coffee cup. "Let's go see." And as Jeremiah had done for three years past, Monroe allowed Claire to lead him out the door.

Victoria and I let them go. I went back to the morning ham and Vee went on with her biscuits. If Claire needed answers on Jeremiah's health, her two sisters would be of little assistance. The sum total of what we knew about horses could be confined in a thimble. Best to let Monroe handle the crisis, since he seemed willing. Surely he would know a way to get Jeremiah on his feet again.

Just then, Mr. Edwards came into the kitchen with his hat in one hand and James on the other. He patiently settled James into the chair Monroe had recently vacated. As I poured them coffee, I remembered what Monroe had mentioned about Mr. Edwards's prowess with the reluctant mule. We could use any help in a pinch. We were totally dependent on Jeremiah's goodwill and good health to take us anywhere off Oak Creek. Beyond that, however, Claire was especially attached to him as she'd taken up the greater part of his daily care.

"Do you know anything about horses, Mr. Edwards?" I asked.

"Ma'am?" he replied as he lifted his cup for a sip of hot coffee.

"Claire has just come in and said that our horse, Jeremiah, is down. She and Monroe have gone to check on him. I wondered if you might have some knowledge of illness in horses?"

"Nothin' to speak of," he answered, "but I'll go take a look." Putting his hat on, he took his coffee and headed for the barn.

The major part of an hour passed before I followed him. Breakfast was ready to be put on the table and no one had come back to the house to report any news of Jeremiah. As I stepped into the early morning shadows of the barn, I saw that someone had lit an oil lamp. Claire, Mr. Edwards, and Monroe were gathered in the last stall around a prostrate Jeremiah. Monroe was speaking as I approached.

"Miss Claire, it happens like this sometimes. Something just strikes 'em down like a hammer. If Jeremiah were younger in years he might fight it off. As it is . . . I don't know how to help him."

I heard Claire sob then try to stifle the sound. I hurried forward to find her huddled in the straw next to Jeremiah's head. The old horse's eyes were closed, but his wheezing breath gave evidence that he still lived. Monroe looked up at me with a clear message in his eyes. Jeremiah was dying. He'd obviously not had the heart to tell Claire straight out. I suppose that would rightly be left up to me.

As if to verify Monroe's words, Jeremiah let out a long labored breath and his front legs trembled. Claire put a comforting hand on his neck as I slipped past Monroe and sat down next to her. She was trembling as hard as the old horse.

"I think we should just watch him for a while, see what he's up to," Mr. Edwards added.

"Shouldn't we try again to get him up?" Claire asked Monroe.

"I don't think we can. Maybe if we wait he'll be stronger later." Monroe didn't sound hopeful so I took charge of my sister's grief.

"Come into the house for a while and warm up. Breakfast is ready. We can't have you getting sick, too," I said, rubbing a hand along her cold arm.

"But I can't leave him out here alone," she answered, combing her fingers through Jeremiah's sparse forelock.

"I'll stay with him," Mr. Edwards offered. "Ya'll go on in and eat. Samson and I will talk his ears off until he'll want to get up and run away just to git some peace."

Claire hesitated and I took the initiative of standing and bringing her up with me. "Thank you, Mr. Edwards."

"Yes, thank you," Claire said dully. "I'll be back in a little bit." She bent and gave Jeremiah a pat on his jaw. "I'll be right back," she said for his benefit.

I hooked an arm around Claire's waist and led her toward the house. Monroe walked on my other side. In the kitchen, with Monroe watching gravely, I helped Claire wash her hands as I used to do when she was younger. Then Monroe washed his own. On the way to breakfast, Claire, in front of me, had pushed through the door into the house when I felt Monroe's hand on my sleeve.

"Go on in," I said to Claire. "We'll be right there."

In a state of shock, she followed my suggestion and a moment later arrived into Victoria's care.

Monroe didn't mince any words. "I don't believe your Jeremiah will last the night."

I felt an odd pain at hearing the news. I had been taught to believe there's always hope, but Monroe sounded certain, and I had yet to find a reason to doubt him in anything. I thought of the many times Jeremiah had willingly if not happily done our bidding, carried us and our burdens. Even though he'd been passed over by needy soldiers, he'd sustained us and had been our only link to an outside world embroiled in a war.

"Well" was the extent of my reaction. I thought if I said anything else I might cry and upset Claire even more before the inevitable would have to be faced.

"If he starts to suffer unduly, I can shoot him, put him out of his pain —"

Although I knew he was being humane, and suggesting a remedy my own father might have proposed, my feelings must have shown on my face because he didn't press the point.

"Otherwise, we'll just wait him out."

I nodded — the sum total of what I could manage at the moment, then pushed through the door to join the others.

The day seemed darker from then on. Victoria and I worked on the laundry while Claire watched over Jeremiah, sometimes with Monroe, sometimes with Arliss Edwards. In the late afternoon, before supper, Monroe and Mr. Edwards with the rest of us in the barn for moral support, made one last effort to coax Jeremiah to his feet. But the old horse couldn't accommodate our hopes. After expending what appeared to be the last of his strength, he settled back onto the ground, his breath heaving then growing weaker as we watched.

Claire, with tears streaming down her face, ran for the house and I, along with Victoria, went after her. It took the rest of the evening to calm her down with cool lavender scented compresses and soothing voices. Finally, after fighting valiantly, she fell asleep in her bed looking as forlorn as the morning I'd found her crying about her lack of a future. Her last sleepy words asked us to pray for a miracle, and I promised her I would but without the prospect of hope. We'd lost so much in the last years, our parents, William and James, our security, our world, now the passing of old Jeremiah seemed like the final blow. Everything must and would be different forever more, and we would have to face what the future held.

Lying in my own bed that night my errant thoughts went back to the evening before, when I'd felt so uplifted by Monroe's words about the spirits looking after us. At the moment I felt too besieged by the day's events to recall the freedom from care I'd experienced. The best I could accomplish on my promise to Claire in Jeremiah's behalf was to ask the spirits to comfort him and lead him to the greener pastures he deserved after serving us so well.

Several hours later I awakened to the sound of creaking stairs. Since the sound moved downward, it wasn't hard to speculate on whose steps I'd heard. Carefully, so as not to wake up Victoria, I slipped from the bed and hastily pulled on whatever clothes and shoes I could find in the dark. Then I followed Claire.

The scene in the barn was much the same as the last time I had ventured inside. Though this time it was Monroe sitting on an overturned oak bucket at Jeremiah's head and Claire in her flannel nightdress, made barely decent by her long woolen cape that had grown too short for her, crouched just outside the stall. Mr. Edwards, relieved from his shift of the vigil, was wrapped in his blankets sleeping soundly.

"You know, when I was in the army," I heard Monroe say, "I saw some horses that were braver than many a man wearing a uniform. Noble beasts for certain, who would stand in the face of the enemy's guns or charge through a hail of bullets any sane man would fear. And, all for the love of their master."

Claire remained silent, but it was obvious she hung on each inspiring word. I stopped just outside the circle of light to listen rather than intrude.

"Old Jeremiah here has served nobly behind the lines, shouldering the responsibility of working this farm and helping you and your sisters. I believe he's about worn himself out doin' his part."

I heard Claire sniff and had to press my fingers against my own lips lest I join her in tears.

"But now, I think he knows you can get by without him and I believe he's looking toward his own rest. It's only fitting,"

Monroe declared as he ran a hand over Jeremiah's neck. "Every old soldier knows when it's time to stay down. And resting after a long, hard road is sweeter than natural sleep."

"But he was putting on some weight since you came and we could feed him better . . ." Claire persisted in a small voice.

"Well then, you can say he got some of his reward for working on low rations. Every soldier appreciates a good meal, even if it might be his last. You and Jeremiah did the best you could for each other, there's no doubt of that."

Claire moved closer to Jeremiah and ran a hand over his muzzle. "How long do you think?" she asked, leaving out any final words like death.

Monroe watched Claire for a moment, gauging her mood I supposed, then he answered, "A few more hours, maybe sunrise, not much longer."

Claire leaned over her prostrate old companion and kissed the side of his jaw. "Thank you, Jeremiah, for being my friend. I hope God grants you acres of green grass and all the cool, clear water you can hold."

Tears rolled down my cheeks as I watched my young sister straighten her back and face

Monroe. "Do you mind if I stay with him?"

Without hesitation, Monroe nodded and stood, allowing her to assume his seat on the bucket. As she settled herself, Monroe noticed me in the dark. He waited, not giving me away, and I made the decision to leave them be. Monroe had done a better job than I at explaining Jeremiah's impending death. There was nothing constructive I could add.

I raised a hand in acknowledgment and thanks before leaving Claire in Monroe's capable company and making my way back to bed.

By the morning, Jeremiah had left us. When I entered the kitchen as the first rooster was crowing, I found Claire, Monroe, and Mr. Edwards huddled around the stove drinking coffee in silence.

"He's gone," Claire said evenly, as though she'd cried out her ration of tears. Her gaze shifted to Monroe. "He didn't suffer, his spirit just slipped away."

I had the feeling those were Monroe's words she'd repeated for my benefit, but they were comforting nonetheless. "Poor old Jeremiah," I added, moving to Claire's side. After giving her a hug I leaned close to her ear. "Why don't you go upstairs to freshen up and dress while we get breakfast ready. You must be worn out. I'll gather the eggs and bring in the water."

Claire nodded and slowly rose from the straight-backed chair. "I think I'll do that," she said.

All of us watched as she left the room, still in grief but having accepted the outcome she'd hoped to avoid. Our Claire was growing into her womanhood in many harsh ways, but she seemed to be holding up.

As soon as the door closed behind her, Mr. Edwards spoke. "Don't worry ma'am. I brought in the eggs and water. I figured you ladies had enough to look after."

"Thank you," I said and began stoking the fire in the firebox in preparation to cook. My gratitude ran deeper than for the chores that had been completed, however. "I also want to thank both of you for helping Claire through this troublesome event. I don't know what we would have done if we'd been here alone."

Both men nodded but didn't speak. I went on, pulling down pans and spooning lard into a bowl. I had just unwrapped the cloth around a hunk of fat-back bacon when Monroe claimed my attention.

"We have another problem though," he

said, sounding reluctant to deliver more bad news.

I stopped with the knife balanced over the meat. "What is that?"

Monroe's reluctance made me worry about what he intended to tell me. But before my fears got the best of me, he sighed and went on. "We have to get Jeremiah, what's left of him, out of the barn. It's wintertime and all, but we can't leave him there."

The enormity of the task nearly made me gasp. If Jeremiah had gone to his eternal rest when Victoria, Claire, and I had been on Oak Creek alone, we would have had no help or advice and would probably have had to desert the barn altogether as a mausoleum for a dead horse we couldn't move. Not a pleasant prospect.

"How in the world will we do that?" I asked.

"Arliss and I are working it out. I just wanted to warn you it might not be a process Miss Claire should witness. We can't very well lift him up and carry him.

"And we'll need to dig a place to bury him, otherwise . . ."

I held up a hand, seeing a picture in my mind's eye of the disintegration that would easily put me off breakfast, not only for this morning, for the next as well. "I understand. Tell me what you wish for me to do. I can occupy Claire and keep her in the house. Perhaps she'll not want to see any more than she has."

Monroe nodded. "After breakfast we're going to set to work. First I imagine we need to dig. You could ask Miss Claire where she might like him put, but keep in mind, we won't be able to take him far."

"Leave it to Victoria and me."

"Julia, would it be too blasphemous to give Jeremiah a funeral?" Claire asked. We'd taken her aside after breakfast, and as delicately as possible, explained what would happen next to her old friend.

I had long ago given up on what might have been considered proper by social standards of a society that had been wiped out by the cruel reality of war and survival. If a funeral for a horse to ease the heart of my sister was a heathen act, then I would take the matter up with my maker on my own judgment day.

"I don't believe we could convince Reverend Pembroke to officiate. However, if you wish to have a service for Jeremiah, then we shall have one."

Victoria voiced her agreement. "You

might ask James when he comes in for a fitting passage to eulogize Jeremiah. He used to be quite good at finding the proper verse for any occasion." A sad expression dimmed her features briefly, no doubt remembering her husband as he had been. "Although you may have to coax him."

The men — Mr. Edwards, Monroe, and James — had adjourned to the barn after breakfast to discuss the task of removing Jeremiah to a better resting place. We finished the last of our laundry chores waiting for some word. Claire had chosen a burial spot a short walk from the house, between our Mother's neglected rose garden and the fields Jeremiah had roamed in his younger years. The ground would be softer there, and the short spell of fair weather would make digging easier. It would still be a long process, no doubt.

"I think," I said to Claire, as I pressed down the last folded bedsheet on top of the pile, "you should take a nap before you undertake any actual funeral arrangements. The men will be busy enough today and you were awake most of the night." I put my hand over hers and squeezed. "Your mind will be clearer and you'll be better able to express your true feelings."

I hoped she would accept my suggestion

231

because I had more than one motive for making it. She did need the rest. There were already faint dark circles of weariness and woe under her eyes, and she seemed more listless than even grief could justify. I also wanted her out of earshot and eyesight of whatever means that had to be invoked to remove Jeremiah from his stall and into his chosen plot.

"I thought I might go out and check on —"

I held up a firm hand to stop her. "I promised Monroe we would stay out of their way in this endeavor. It's not an easy or pleasant task and having to worry about our safety and sensibilities is too much to ask of volunteers."

It seems I had gotten more adept at lying because Claire's gaze dropped and she sighed. "You're right. I'm not sure I want to see."

Silently congratulating my sister on her good sense, I ran a hand along her shoulders. "Go upstairs and get some rest, Sweet. I'll call you if there is need. Do you want me to come up and see you safe under the covers?"

Claire didn't answer, so I took that as a yes. "Let's go then."

After tucking Claire in as I had done a

thousand times in her childhood, I kissed her cheek and prepared to leave her to her rest.

"You were right about Sergeant Tacy — Monroe," Claire said sleepily. "He's a good man. Nothing to be afraid of. . . ."

A good man, of that I felt assured.

As her tired eyes fluttered shut, I glanced past the bed and spied the unfinished wedding dress hanging inside out on a peg behind a newer dress in the wardrobe. I crossed the room and pulled it free.

"He would make some lucky woman a fine husband, don't you think?" I said, keeping the conversation going in hopes of firmly planting the idea in her sleepy head.

"Hmmm, mmmm," she replied, which I took as agreement. I reversed the dress, brushed the folds of the pristine material we'd worked so diligently over and shook the closet wrinkles loose. Satisfied that I had at least brought the subject up, I returned the dress to a new peg so it would be the first thing Claire saw when she awoke. Perhaps Jeremiah's demise had accomplished what Victoria and I had not been able to do — bringing Claire and Monroe together on common ground.

Chapter Fourteen

"At least the ground isn't frozen," Arliss Edwards said as he dropped the armload of spades and pitchforks he'd carried from the barn, before picking up one rusty but sturdy tool to use. Monroe chose the only other spade with a complete handle and moved to the designated spot to dig.

"Someone please hand me a shovel," James said stiffly, holding out his hand in expectation. Neither Victoria nor I moved, though I glanced at Mr. Edwards.

"I had to dig graves blind or not when I was in Camp Chase," James said, insistence in his voice.

Arliss nodded to me and I bent to find a suitable tool. The only one left with a proper handle was a pitchfork. The sharp tines would at least break the ground and the grass. I straightened to hand it to James, but Mr. Edwards interrupted.

"Here, Mr. James, you take this shovel." Mr. Edwards placed the tool in James's grasp then took his other arm to guide him forward. When they reached a place near Monroe, Mr. Edwards let go of James and he began to dig. All the rest of us could do was stand back and watch. The first shovelful of dirt landed on Monroe's boots. He continued to dig without comment. The second dirt clod landed at Victoria's feet and sent a spray of sandy residue against her hemline.

Understanding dawned of why Mr. Edwards had thought a shovel rather than a pitchfork would be the safer choice when dealing with a blind man, and I felt an inappropriate bubble of laughter forming in my throat. After the sadness and sleeplessness of the prior evening, I didn't trust my ability to control it so I pressed a hand over my mouth and avoided anyone's gaze.

The next shovelful hit Monroe directly in the knees, and he stopped digging. I had to turn away lest I give in to a very unladylike guffaw. I heard Victoria make a suspicious sound like a cough before I found myself facing Arliss again.

"To the left, Mr. James," Mr. Edwards said, trying not to betray the smile on his face. "Dig and throw to the left."

James, without argument or understanding of what he'd done, agreeably shifted his aim. Even so, Monroe waited for the next shovelful to miss him before going back to work. Victoria, her cheeks pinker than a nosegay of sweet peas, shook out her skirts and announced the dinner menu of beans and ham before taking my arm and tugging me toward the house.

As Claire slept, Victoria and I carried on with our chores and made our hopeful plans to finish the wedding dress when she awoke. I shared Claire's sleepy declaration about Monroe, and it had an uplifting effect on us both. Victoria, ever the skeptic, even allowed that perhaps we'd received the answers to our prayers after all. Unfortunately it had come in the form of Jeremiah's death, but we were willing to trade one sadness for Claire's ultimate happiness.

The men dug until dinnertime, when they were over waist deep in a plot big enough for a horse. We served them food outside since they were covered in dirt and had more dirty work to do before sunset. They ate without conversation, using the same mechanical precision with which they'd dug, then put down their empty plates before heading to the barn.

The part I had dreaded had arrived. Lacking the personal expertise of farmwork or any kind of heavy labor, my imagination could not form a picture of how three men, one of them blind, might move the dead weight of an animal of Jeremiah's stature. He'd been old and rangy but solid. I'd found that out when I'd harnessed him once and he'd shifted his weight with one of his feet coming to rest on top of my own. I'd pushed and shouted, even struck him on the shoulder before he caught on to my distress and moved. He was as weighty and as slow to motion as a locomotive, and he lacked the convenience of wheels. I could only hope that some manly computation of weights and measures would suffice to move him.

I went back to cleaning dishes and tried to clear my mind of any but mundane thoughts. The death of an old friend was bad enough without the attendant details of a burden that must be carried, literally. I had cleaned and rearranged the kitchen from top shelf to floorboards when I heard a shout in the yard. Unable to resist my morbid curiosity, I went to the kitchen door, which faced the barn, and opened it.

The barn doors had been swung wide. The bright afternoon sun reflecting off the weathered wood made it difficult to see into the gloom of the interior. I waited as I could hear more commotion. After several moments, I could see Monroe's horse with him beside it, both harnessed and pulling like two oxen. As they slowly moved ahead into the sun, the horse worried at the unfamiliar task and it took every bit of Monroe's attention to keep him in a forward motion.

Then I saw James and Arliss Edwards, tethered to either side of Samson, the newly christened reluctant mule. Mr. Edwards kept up a steady stream of compliments and nonsense obviously meant for the mule with an occasional instruction for the rest to keep the pulling consistent. As the men and the animals strained step by step, literally foot by foot, their burden, Jeremiah, moved into the sunshine.

"Step up there, Samson," Mr. Edwards crooned as he labored on the mule's left side. Samson appeared to be listening. He put his head down, his ears back and pulled. "You're the strongest and the handsomest mule that walks the Earth. You're the twinkle in your mama's eye, the dream of all the ladies, first prize for any farmer. Step up!"

I might have smiled at his nonsense but I heard the door to the house behind me open and close and my attention scattered. Thinking it was Victoria, I didn't turn. But it was Claire who moved up next to me in the open doorway. I heard a small gasping sound, then she went still. Too late to prevent the scene before her, I slipped an arm around her waist and pulled her close. She rested her head on my shoulder, remained silent and watched.

Jeremiah had cleared the barn. After all the pulling he'd done in his lifetime, he was the one calm participant in this monumental effort. His work was done. He looked almost peaceful, certainly oblivious to his pallbearers. The procession advanced another five or six feet, the rhythmic sound of Mr. Edwards's voice keeping everyone in time until he announced a planned turn to the left.

"Mr. Monroe, start the turn," Arliss said.

Monroe, tethered to his horse, began crowding him to the left, shoulder to shoulder. The horse, obviously used to being led, not driven, shied sideways, dragging Monroe with him before rearing and tangling one foot in the ropes. Unable to do anything else, I held my breath and hoped the horse wouldn't do any damage to the living before the dead could be attended.

"Whoa, there," Monroe coaxed and put

a steadying hand on the horse's halter, but the animal reared again, frantic because his leg was caught. This time he nearly sat on his haunches before his leg came free and his hoof knocked Monroe's hat into the dirt.

The procession came to a halt.

Without explanation, Claire left my side, went down the stairs into the side yard and moved to the head of the horse Monroe was trying to calm. She gathered the horse's halter in one hand, pulled his head down, and spoke low and soothingly to the trembling animal. I couldn't hear her words, but Monroe's grumbling sound of exasperation as he bent to retrieve his hat reached me loud and clear. I followed my sister into the yard.

"I'll lead him," Claire announced. "He knows me well enough."

Monroe looked to me, for concurrence I suppose, before saying, "You could get hurt Miss Claire. He's likely to step all over both of us before we're done."

Claire kept her eyes off Jeremiah and on the problem horse who seemed a good bit calmer. "I'm not afraid of him," she declared, then gazed at me to see if I would support her or disagree. I could see the determination in her eyes, the plea. She needed to help. Hurt or not, I would not stop her.

"I'll get a lead rope from the barn," I offered. Better to have her at the end of a short rope than under the horse's head clinging to a halter.

As I returned from my errand, I saw that Victoria had come to stand on the steps outside the kitchen door. She had one hand resting over her heart, and I knew she might have protested had she come out sooner and discovered our intent. Too late for that now. Monroe fastened the rope and reluctantly handed it to Claire.

"If he gets uppity again, I expect you to get out of the way and let me handle him," he said. "Promise you'll do that."

Claire nodded.

Monroe looked over his shoulder toward Arliss Edwards and nodded. "Let me get Samson started first, Miss Claire, then lead him to the left," Mr. Edwards instructed. "We need a wide turn."

Claire bobbed her head once more and wrapped the rope twice around the fingers of one hand. Without speaking, Monroe took her arm, unwrapped the rope, coiled it and handed it back. "Hold it, don't wrap it. If he goes up, let go."

Monroe stared at me gravely, and I knew

he would do his best to keep Claire from harm. I moved out of the way and went to stand with Victoria.

"Step up there, handsome man," Mr. Edwards said, beginning his nonsense speak once more.

The mule obediently began to pull, James and Mr. Edwards beside him.

"All right, Miss Claire."

Claire, taking a cue from Mr. Edwards, used her voice as she tugged the horse forward. "Come. Let's go for a walk," she said in a coaxing voice.

The horse planted his feet and refused to move. Monroe, next to him, strained forward to give him the right idea. Claire pulled again, making a sort of kissing sound. The horse made one effort then shied backward. Of a sudden, Claire seemed to get another idea. She turned her back to the horse as one would when leading him normally. "Let's go boy," she said, seemingly oblivious to her vulnerable position.

My heart pounded frantically. Victoria, who'd been a silent observer, slipped her hand into mine and squeezed hard.

"Step up, boy, step up," Mr. Edwards continued, his voice sounding more strained than cajoling.

As if he'd received the dawn of understanding, the horse's head came down to its natural position and he took one hesitant step forward, then another. Claire did not look back or ask for direction, she led him into the turn and Jeremiah was six feet closer to his final resting place.

The work continued without incident for another three quarters of an hour. Victoria and I followed the slow moving procession to the grave site, thinking the worst had passed.

We were wrong.

"Miss Claire, you take that horse along the right side of the hole, we'll go to the left."

It seemed logical enough to me. The people and animals in the harness would split ranks and go around the grave, then pull Jeremiah straight into it.

"Lead him from the right shoulder," Monroe cautioned and I began to see the potential for disaster. Claire moved as she'd been told, leading the horse wide to the right, away from the hole. The horse began to toss his head in mounting distress.

"He's afraid of it," Claire said. Although the words sounded calm, I could see she was worried. Without permission, she changed hands and switched sides, walking between the skittish horse and a hole several feet deep. The horse settled slightly although he was blowing and walleyed.

Victoria's grip on my hand threatened to crush my fingers. Monroe began to untangle himself from the harness, I suppose to take Claire's place. The horse was abreast of the grave site now, with Mr. Edwards, James, and Samson on the opposite side. Jeremiah was five feet from his home for eternity when Monroe's horse decided he'd had enough.

He reared and grunted as he went over backward. Monroe barely got clear as the horse fell to the ground. He'd pulled the rope from Claire's hands and struggled sideways. My fear of Claire falling in the grave and being crushed by the reluctant horse was replaced by a new and unexpected calamity.

As the horse thrashed sideways and Monroe tried to control him, the mule, along with James and Mr. Edwards, was being dragged toward the hole. Victoria gasped as James's feet slipped on the edge of the grave and he lost his footing.

Arliss Edwards had the presence of mind to clasp James's groping arm and with herculean strength hauled him up, halfway across the mule's back and held him there.

"Pull, Samson!" Mr. Edwards ordered as he leaned away from the mule and the hole they were being dragged toward. "Come on, big man! Save us up out of here!"

The mule, his feet planted against the pull of the larger, struggling horse, teetered on the brink, holding his weight and James's. Victoria gasped and turned her face into my shoulder. I could only stand frozen. If they fell, we would most likely lose James for a second time and permanently.

Shouting and waving his arms, Monroe gave up trying to calm the horse. He drove him back toward the grave to take the strain off the harness and give Samson a chance to gain purchase. In another tense moment, the crisis was over. Samson managed to retain his footing and dragged James from the brink of certain disaster. James, Mr. Edwards, and the worn-out, tangled horse all fell to the Earth, breathing hard. The mule stood his ground.

Victoria left my comfort and went toward her husband. I followed. Monroe took a moment to pull a knife from his pocket and cut the line connecting the horse to Jeremiah and Samson's harness.

Then, he walked over to the heroic mule and removed his hat in what looked like a gesture of respect.

"I will never say another unkind word to you or about you," Monroe promised solemnly. Then he replaced his hat and helped James to his feet. "Are you all right Mr. James?"

James, sweaty and dirty, had the temerity to smile. "I am well. And, please don't tell me what just almost happened. My imagination is working well enough."

Monroe extended his hand to Mr. Edwards and pulled him to his feet. "I hadn't thought this chore would kill us all," Monroe said. "But if I ever have to do something like this again, I would hope you're on my flank."

Mr. Edwards looked perplexed for a moment, unused to compliments it seemed. Then he gave Samson a solid pat on the shoulder. "Was this handsome mule that saved us, Mr. Monroe."

"But it was you who saved James," Victoria spoke up. "Thank you Mr. Edwards."

He nodded. "You're welcome, ma'am. Mr. James and I have been through some things. I didn't come all this way to let him get flattened if I could help it."

I heard Claire's voice then and glanced

in her direction. I'd forgotten her in the melee. She'd coaxed Monroe's horse to his feet and was removing the remaining harness. The horse was lathered and dripping sweat in the cool air, but he didn't seem to be injured.

"We're going to have to do this without the horse," Monroe declared.

"Perhaps you should wait and try again tomorrow," Victoria suggested, studying her husband with worried eyes.

"We got him pretty close, we should be able to pull him the rest of the way," Arliss said. "Better we go on now and maybe get it done."

It took another hour and a half of back-breaking work, but Jeremiah finally reached his destination. Victoria, Claire, and I returned to the house to finish preparing a victory supper while the men shoveled dirt to fill the grave. They came back to the house filthy, tired, and looking satisfied with a job well done.

Hallelujah.

That was when I had my inspiration. Claire and I dragged out the hip bath, took it round the house to the parson's room, and then started hauling water. Inside, Victoria moved the beans, smoked venison, and corn mush to the back of the stove and used both our large kettles to heat bath-water. The weather had remained warmer than usual for this time of year so bathing would not be torture and might even ease tired limbs. A bath and supper was the sum total of what we could afford to pay the men for their labors. Since we were out of flour, we fed them cornmeal ashcakes and the last of our watered-down coffee while they waited for their turn in the bathwater.

Shortly after supper, Monroe and Arliss Edwards, looking done-in, took their leave to get some much earned rest. James, how-ever, seemed more animated than usual and insisted that Claire read to him so they might find a passage fitting for the funeral of Jeremiah. Victoria joined them. As for myself, after such a taxing day I decided a good night's sleep would be the best medi-cine for body and soul so I went upstairs.

After unpinning and brushing my hair, I undressed and snuggled between the cool, clean sheets, weighted down by quilts, with the intention of immediate and dreamless sleep. But, as I lay in the darkness, I found that my mind remained tangled in the events of the waking world. Portraits of Monroe struggling with his terrified horse, of the men bent and pulling Jeremiah like beasts of burden, of James teetering on the brink of life and death with no one to help but the stubbornness of a mule, kept me awake and troubled. It had been a hard day for each of us in his own way, but something else, some deeper meaning jostled for my attention.

Then with the suddenness of a sword thrust, I met the truth. I had briefly touched on it prior, wondering what my sisters and I would have done if we'd been alone to deal with Jeremiah's demise. What I hadn't realized then, and did now with full clarity, was that soon we would be alone again. Monroe, whether he took a fancy for our Claire or not, would have to return to Savannah and his family business. Arliss Edwards had his own family to find. That would leave three women and a blind man to run the farm.

We surely would starve.

Not only that, we might kill ourselves trying to work the land and still starve. Oak Creek would have to be sold. Not because we lacked the spirit or the will, but because physically, we could not reestablish a farm that had required five regular field hands and ten additional ones during harvest. We had no money to hire labor as our father had done. We had no husbands to work the land. As of yesterday, we didn't even have a horse to harness to a plow.

Tears welled in my eyes. Deep in my moment of dismal discovery I felt a thankfulness that we had not realized before how desperate our situation had grown. My sisters and I might have faded and given up rather than survived the last two years. The question to be answered now was not whether we would leave Oak Creek, but when and how.

The entire South had been broken. Land was being sold for any fraction of its worth, many times simply for the price of taxes owed. The notion of losing Oak Creek for a pittance tightened my throat. Surely the earthly spirit of my part-Scots father would fly out of his grave with a howl to see his family's land reduced in such a manner. And on the other side of the pain in losing our only home, we would have to face the world with little or no resources. I began to see the point James valiantly tried to make when he'd first arrived. He might be blind and unable to do a man's work, but he had a small pension. My sisters and I were in a more untenable position. We were women without the protection of marriage and family. We'd be forced to rely on charity from distant and decidedly uncharitable family members like our cousins the Langhorns or worse, from complete strangers.

I put a hand over my hammering heart and felt the shape of William's wedding ring on its chain beneath my nightdress. Whether William had sent spirits to protect us or not, they couldn't work the farm or hunt for meat, or pay the taxes. Determination beat back my fear. I would go to William's family and beg, if necessary, for my sisters and myself. Surely they couldn't refuse us some sort of help. I would not let them.

Looking back, I realized how foolish and impractical our whimsical wedding dress plan had been. We couldn't construct a dress then sit and wait to find Claire a husband, we had to act and soon. If only Claire could see the urgency, understand the danger of her diminished future at Oak Creek, and see that she alone could take steps to save herself. But, I despaired of being able to convince her.

That's when I decided to act outright, to ask Monroe to marry my sister. There was no time to waste. Surely he would grasp the gravity of the situation. He'd been our savior so far, and if his heart wasn't committed elsewhere, he must consider the possibility of making a match with a young, pretty wife who would give him sons and oversee his home as a viable one. I might have to threaten Claire in order to overcome her reluctance. Threats, however, seemed like the lessor evil to starvation and destitution.

For some unaccountable reason, it had become increasingly difficult for me to envision Claire and Monroe together. Perhaps it was because I knew Claire's mind, even though lately she seemed to have had a change of heart. I could only hope she would come around. I made a firm resolve for the three of us to finish Claire's wedding dress the next day. As soon as the circle was complete, then I would approach Monroe with my proposal.

I remained awake, fencing with my fears, until Victoria opened the door to the bedroom. I pretended to be asleep when she entered to keep myself from pouring out my worries to her. No use for both of us to agonize until our obvious lack of a future required it.

When I finally reached exhaustion and drifted off, thankfully my fears deserted me. I dreamed of fields of corn and some other crop that I did not recognize. Abundance. In the dream I kicked off my shoes and ran between the rows completely hidden by the tall greenery. Then my steps slowed as I approached my mother's rose garden, which, unlike the present, flourished in full bloom. This welcome vision of better days filled my heart with love and longing. I refused to think of the cruelty of this brief visit to the past when the future loomed like the blade of a guillotine over our heads.

I half expected to see my mother clipping the heavily scented buds to grace her Sunday dinner table, or possibly even William riding up the drive on his big bay stallion. Anything wonderful seemed likely. But as I gazed toward the drive willing my heart's wish, Monroe appeared wearing shirtsleeves and suspenders. He waved from the far corner of the house and I waved back before he disappeared.

I awoke with new energy. The dream had not only calmed my fears but had reinforced my conviction that Monroe must marry Claire. He had to be the key to restoring Oak Creek, or at least he would save my younger sister and leave me to worry over Victoria and James.

I kicked off the covers and faced the new day refreshed by the past and resolved to a better future.

Chapter Fifteen

The weather had turned cold again during the night, reminding us that one unseasonable spate of mild temperatures did not mean the arrival of spring. The funeral for Jeremiah was a solemn affair, although not as sad as his passing. Dressed in our newer dresses, with coal-scuttle bonnets, capes, scarves, and bowed heads, Victoria and I followed Claire's lead as we proceeded to say good-bye to our old friend. Claire spoke on Jeremiah's behalf, numbering the tasks he had undertaken at our bidding, listing the ways he'd shared our hardships and our happier times, and wishing him Godspeed in his journey to "horse heaven."

I had no opinion on where or how horses might populate the spirit world, although I had experienced the vision of some who seemed to have ended up in an opposite direction. The earthbound ones who still marched to war with their restless, ghostly masters would certainly be awarded little rest or care until they reached the end of their stamina, or a brighter path.

With her final tribute faltering and after the judicious use of her handkerchief, Claire called on James to speak. She had just guided him to the head of the grave when the neighing of a horse and the sound of hooves and buggy wheels reached us in the cold morning air. I thought for a moment we might in truth witness Jeremiah's spiritual journey, perhaps pulling a winged chariot. After our recent invasion by spirits on all sides, nothing less would have surprised me. But when I turned, I saw Reverend Pembroke stepping down from his carriage and watched as he tethered his horse to the porch rail before waving and moving toward us.

He approached our heathen ceremony with a worried air and his bible clutched in his hands. There was no time to consider a proper lie. In a moment, he was upon us.

"Who has passed?" he asked, winded, and appearing as though he believed he'd arrived just in time for our spiritual emergency.

The men, hats respectfully in hands, looked to me for an answer and Claire remained mute. "It is our old horse, Jeremiah," I informed him. I did my best to pretend that it was perfectly normal for us to be bidding a horse such a formal adieu.

"A horse?" Reverend Pembroke asked, obviously perplexed.

"Yes," I continued. "He was a hard worker and our Claire's friend." My tone gave him no foothold for argument and to complement my words, Claire moved next to me and took my arm. United was the face of our resoluteness. He wavered.

"I see. Well, do go on. I apologize for interrupting."

Claire squeezed my arm, in triumph I supposed, before asking James to continue. The Reverend removed his own hat, crossed protective hands over his bible as though he might hide it from our blasphemy and stood between Victoria and myself.

James, wearing his brushed and repaired coat, neck cloth, and waistcoat with his spectacles in the breast pocket, opened a book as though he intended to read. He said something low and probably reassuring to Claire before she moved away. Then he began to speak, never once glancing at the open book he held before him.

"We have come to honor a noble beast. One who spent his days in toil without discord and who suffered the privations of war alongside his masters.

"On this sad occasion, I would defer to Tennyson —" James cleared his throat and struck the stance of a poet. He looked so like his old self before the war that my heart warmed with the memory.

"The path by which we twain did go,
Which led by tracts that pleased us well,
Thro' four sweet years arose and fell,
From flower to flower, from snow to snow.

And we with singing cheer'd the way,
And, crown'd with all the season lent,
From April on to April went,
And glad at heart from May to May.

But where the path we walk'd began
To slant the fifth autumnal slope,
As we descended following Hope,
There sat the Shadow fear'd of man.

Who broke our fair companionship,
And spread his mantle dark and cold,
And wrapt thee formless in the fold,
And dull'd the murmur on thy lip.

And bore thee where I could not see
Nor follow, tho' I walk in haste,

And think, that somewhere in the waste
The Shadow sits and waits for me."

I heard a muffled sob emanate from Victoria, so affected by James's resplendent voice, I felt much of the same mind. Although the question rose in me whether Victoria grieved for Jeremiah or for her blind husband who, holding a book from habit, recited poetry from his heart's memory as he had done in happier days.

Soon, James went on.

"William Shakespeare had said of a horse, 'When I bestride him, I soar, I am a hawk; He trots the air; The earth sings when he touches it; The basest horn of his hoof is more musical than the piper of Hermes. He is pure air and fire.' "

James closed the book in his hands and stared into a clear, cold sky he couldn't see. "Here Lord, lies Jeremiah. Take him into your ark and give him ease. He has done well by his life and deserves your peace."

He bowed his head and fell silent. The wind pushed a few wintered leaves along the cold, newly churned ground at our feet as we each said our final, silent good-byes. A few moments later, Reverend Pembroke cleared his throat. Seemingly called upon to say something, he moved to stand next to James, opened his bible, and began to recite.

"For as much as it has pleased Almighty God to take out of this world the soul of —" He stopped then, looking stumped.

"Jeremiah," Claire prompted.

The Reverend cleared his throat once more. "The soul of *Jeremiah*, we therefore commit his body to the ground, Earth to Earth, ashes to ashes, dust to dust, looking for that blessed hope when the Lord Himself shall descend from heaven with a shout, with the voice of the archangel, and with the trump of God, and the dead in Christ shall rise first, caught up together with them in the clouds to meet the Lord in the air, and so shall we ever be with the Lord, wherefore comfort ye one another with these words."

Looking relieved to reach the end of a ceremony he'd not foreseen and did not completely approve of, Reverend Pembroke nodded officially and closed his bible. I put an arm around Claire and approached him.

"Come to the house Reverend, we have breakfast waiting on the stove." We walked along with him as Victoria and James followed. Monroe and Mr. Edwards brought up the rear.

"I have not seen you ladies at Sunday service these last few weeks," he said. "I asked your neighbors about your well-being and none of them could enlighten me. So, I took it upon myself to make a visit and see with my own eyes how you are faring."

"We appreciate your concern," I replied, although in the uncharitable part of my mind I wondered if his wife had put him up to it in hopes of having something to report about the Atwater sisters to her circle. "We've had a good many uncommon events happen in the last month and a half," I explained.

"Uncommon events do not outweigh the word of the gospel," the Reverend chided.

By this time we'd reached the front porch steps. I decided it was as good a time as any to introduce our diverse temporary family who'd been the result of our "uncommon events." I turned and waited for the others to catch up.

"Do you remember our brother-in-law, Victoria's husband, James Whitmore?"

James put out his hand in our general direction. After a surprised start of a look, the Reverend took it and shook it briskly.

"Why, sir, we'd heard you'd met your end fighting for the cause," he said. "Even held a fine memorial service in your honor."

"I did meet my end, Reverend. But I appear to live still," James replied.

"And this is Sgt. Monroe Tacy," I continued, giving the Reverend little time to ask any questions. "He was a friend of William's."

"Sergeant," the Reverend acknowledged. He seemed ready to ask the same infernal question about Claire's intended so I flung a hand toward Arliss Edwards.

"This is Mr. Edwards. He saved James's life and has earned our eternal friendship and gratitude."

Mr. Edwards removed his hat but did not reach out to the Reverend. The Reverend seemed of the same mind. He'd frowned over my declaration of "eternal" friendship. "Mr. Edwards," the Reverend acknowledged with a nod of his head.

"Now that we all know each other," Victoria broke in, "Let's get inside out of the cold and have breakfast."

As Claire opened the door for the Reverend, and Victoria with James followed him through it, Mr. Edwards motioned me aside. "I'll be right in," I called to the others before moving down the stairs to stand with Mr. Edwards and Monroe.

"I'd just as soon take my breakfast out in the kitchen if you don't mind, ma'am. I think I caught a chill this morning after that bath last night and I could use a spell in a warm place."

I studied his guileless face for a long moment. He held my gaze but I was on to his game. "You're telling me a tale, aren't you, Mr. Edwards?"

"Well, yes and no, ma'am," he said with reluctance. "The truth is, I can always stand a spell in a warm place. But, I think eating at the table with your preacher would be warmer than I can take."

When I started to disagree, Mr. Edwards stopped me by looking to Monroe for support. "I'll be leaving here soon. There's no need to have anyone even know I was here."

Realizing he was trying to protect my sisters and myself from gossip or worse, I still felt obliged to defend him if need be. Notwithstanding, he'd brought James home to us and saved his life in front of our eyes. I called on the instructive Mrs. Habersham's comportment of the queen. "This is our home, Mr. Edwards. We will bring whomever we wish to our table."

"I believe we'll both take our meal in the kitchen," Monroe said, cutting off my best effort to date at pretending regal authority.

"But —"

"You give the Reverend our regrets and tell him we had some pressing work to attend to. After all, this ain't Sunday. We need to go into town."

Faced with Mr. Edwards's logic and Monroe's support of it, I could do little to persuade otherwise. "Well, I —"

"I know you can convince him to do without us," Monroe finished, leaving me with my mouth open like a snared fish. Then he and Mr. Edwards made their way around the house to the kitchen door.

Later I would be grateful for their decision, but at that moment I felt outmaneuvered and angry. Not with Monroe or Arliss Edwards, but with yet another surprise visitor, Reverend Pembroke, whom I was not prepared to handle. In the end, I decided that making the point of having Mr. Edwards at our table might be a triumph for my pride, but it would most likely bring embarrassment or discomfort to Mr. Edwards himself — the gain hardly worth the price.

Feeling deserted, I entered the house by the front door, passed through the dining room briefly with assurances I would return soon, then joined Claire out in the kitchen to help serve. We left Victoria and James to entertain the Reverend.

Shortly, after eating a hurried breakfast, Mr. Edwards harnessed Samson to the wagon and Monroe mounted his reluctant horse. As they headed into town for much needed supplies, Claire and I returned to the table and our guest.

"It's been quite a long time since I've visited Oak Creek," the Reverend was saying as I sank into my chair. He gazed down at his plate with not a little trepidation. "Not since your mother's funeral service, may she rest in peace."

"Amen," I said, fervently under my breath. I hoped our mother was otherwise occupied with the glory of heaven rather than witnessing how far the genteel hospitality of her home, and the studied if not perfect decorum of her daughters had fallen. We had not even a biscuit to offer the Reverend and only two eggs to make batter. We were reduced to parched rye coffee and tough, cornmeal flapjacks with slivers of ham left over from the previous day's supper.

"I must apologize for Sergeant Tacy and Mr. Edwards, they won't be joining us," I said. "They have some pressing business, which must be attended."

"Will you say grace, Reverend?" Victoria asked, forestalling any questions. If she had any misgivings about the coarseness of the food, or our missing members, they were well hidden. At least it seemed one of us had taken Mrs. Habersham's training to heart.

"Why certainly," the Reverend answered and proceeded to bless our table with the same vigor and volume he might use from his pulpit. "Almighty God in heaven . . ."

Afterward, as I picked up my fork, I could feel my mother's presence in the room. Not her ghost, thank goodness. But something closer to the past, when she'd been alive in this house. Death removed, as if she might walk in from another room at any moment. And, instead of disappointment, the emanation that enveloped me was one of pride. My mother had never been one to suffer self-pity or self-righteousness. I decided that neither should I.

"How is Mrs. Pembroke and your family?" I asked as though we were sitting before an eight-course meal prepared by liveried servants.

The Reverend had just deposited a forkful of molasses-sweetened flapjacks into his greatest asset, his mouth, which required his chewing before he could answer. I waited modestly with an interested expression until he swallowed.

"Why, everyone is doing well," he answered, dabbing his lips with a napkin. "My son will be old enough for seminary school this fall and my two daughters have joined the youth charity group in the church, which my wife has begun." His speculative gaze moved to Claire. "They gather baskets of food-stuffs for the poor. We all must do our part, you know."

The idea that they might be soon gathering a basket for the remaining residents of Oak Creek rattled my composure. I took my time raising my glass for a sip of water before going on.

"You must be very proud of them."

James, who had grown accustomed to the set of our china, at that moment made an uncommon error in placement, nearly setting his coffee cup on top of Victoria's. Without ado or mishap, Vee guided his hand to a proper course before they both went back to the meal. Reverend Pembroke did not miss the exchange.

"So, Mr. Whitmore, when did you return to your home? We must have you come to Sunday services for a proper welcome."

James, who had been studiously lifting a

fork of flapjack to his mouth, paused, the portion on the fork teetering for a moment then falling back onto his plate.

"I've only just arrived a week ago," James replied before putting the empty fork into his mouth. Frowning over the missing food, he lowered the utensil for another attempt. We, of course, were oblivious to James's odd ways. The Reverend Pembroke seemed to require answers.

He leaned closer to me and whispered, "What's wrong with him?"

"I'm blind, not deaf," James said in a loud voice. His sightless stare struck a target somewhere between the coffee pot at the end of the table and the empty chair that Monroe would have normally occupied. Claire raised her napkin to cover, judging by the humor sparkling in her eyes, a smile.

Reverend Pembroke harrumphed once gazing pointedly at the spectacles resting in James's vest pocket. "Excuse me, sir," he stammered. "I didn't mean —"

"I lost the better part of my sight fighting for a bloody river in Georgia," James said, lowering his fork. Any humor lurking at the table disappeared. Victoria's hand came to rest on her husband's wrist. Support or restraint, I could not tell although Victoria had no great respect for the Reverend. He and his wife had grown too fat during the war while many in the county surrounding his church had suffered.

This is when I decided it was better that Monroe and Arliss Edwards had absented themselves from our table. We would have our hands full defending our defiant brother-in-law. Defending Reverend Pembroke from the combined complement of our temporary family would have been beyond my capabilities. As it turned out, any defense was unnecessary. Only words passed between them.

"Thank God you survived, sir," the Reverend said. "By His grace you were delivered —"

"By His grace I'm a half-dead man required to walk the Earth and be a burden to others," James declared. "Where is the mercy in that?"

"God's judgment falls at the end of a life, not at each trial and tribulation. I'm sure there is a purpose in His plan for you."

James uncannily stared directly at the Reverend for the first time. The Reverend appeared to be caught by his sightless yet pointed glower and unable to go on with his usual verbosity.

"Since you know God's mind so well, you ask Him what purpose I can serve," James countered. "I have done so until in the silence I thought my hearing had been taken as well." With an indrawn breath of having said his piece, James patted Victoria's hand before pulling his arm away and resuming his breakfast.

Reverend Pembroke, released by James's intensive attentions, stared for a mere moment, then followed his subject's lead, eating his flapjacks without taking the time to taste them thoroughly.

The remainder of the breakfast passed in small talk about our neighbors and the difficult times ahead. At least the subject of Claire's wedding did not come up straightaway. I suppose since we did not mention it, the Reverend may have thought better of doing so himself. He'd already been taken to task unexpectedly.

"The railway into Danville has been completely repaired," the Reverend reported. "It's been running a regular schedule for the last few weeks."

"Really?" I replied, but my mind for some reason went to Monroe. He'd arrived by rail when that source of travel had been inconstant at best. Now it would be even easier for him to leave us — and on a regular schedule to boot. I lost my appetite for the last remaining flapjack on my plate, which I knew would please our hens who reaped the reward of leftovers. The fear for our future returned with a vengeance. "How do you think our county will hold up under this reconstruction?" I asked. I hoped to hear good news about our neighbors, the people closest to our needs.

The Reverend shook his head. "Since the murder of Lincoln, the government seems to believe any kindness to the South is a weakness to be expunged. There will be no mercy or help from that quarter, and their incessant meddling will invade our lives as surely as their armies did during the fighting." His gaze shifted to Claire. "Why, in order to be married, our spurious military governor demands the intended swear allegiance to the Union and promise to pray for the soul of Abraham Lincoln before the service may be performed."

James and Claire both, and I'm certain for different reasons, squirmed in their seats but remained silent. I, on the other hand, had nothing to lose. "We expect our Claire to be married next month, as soon as her intended returns. After that, those of us who remain plan to rebuild this farm."

The Reverend's gaze skipped around the

table as if to gauge the fortitude of the remaining few. When his eyes descended on me again, they held a look of pity. "Well, if there is anything I can advise you on, feel free to ask. There are many who'll be starting over. As a matter of fact, our family will be moving to what was formerly the Shelton's place over near Glencoe. They found the prospect of beginning again in the midst of Union occupation too daunting. They were outspoken supporters of the war, sending off three sons and a father to fight. All but one returned home, but none had the wish to swear allegiance to their enemies. They have sold out and moved west."

It seemed that my judgmental nature had not been quelled, because I immediately wondered at what price the Reverend had acquired the twelve hundred acres belonging to the old friends of my parents. And was it a "fair" price? It would be too scandalous to ask.

"I hope they find a better place," I said lamely.

"There is no better place," the Reverend declared. "We have reaped the whirlwind and must abide until it passes." His attention arrowed to Claire once more. "Miss Claire, when your intended arrives, you bring him to the church. We can discuss the officiating then." When she only nodded in reply he added, "Don't you worry. I decree we only require the bride and groom pledge allegiance to God and to one another. Your prayers are your own to offer."

By the time Monroe and Arliss Edwards returned from town, we'd been working on Claire's dress for the better part of four hours. To our collective relief, Reverend Pembroke had taken his leave within a barely respectable interval after breakfast. James had remained sitting in a rocker on the front porch as if to guard against any change of heart on the Reverend's part. Before boarding his carriage he'd assured us he would testify to our wellbeing to the community and also encouraged us in no uncertain terms to be in church the following Sunday.

I determined to have this marriage tangle settled by then. To either introduce Monroe as Claire's intended or confess the failure of our plans.

The dress — the wedding dress — was finally complete. We'd hemmed, embroidered, and appliquéd the finishing touches. All we lacked were proper shoes and a willing, flesh-and-blood groom.

I heard the sound of our own wagon coming down the drive as we helped Claire into her dress for a final fitting. It didn't occur to me to hide our occupation until the dining room door swung open and Monroe walked through followed by Arliss Edwards. They both stopped, seemingly stunned at the sight of Claire decked out in her finery. Monroe looked unnatural, as though he'd lost all the air in his lungs. Then he frowned. Not a promising sign.

"We're ready to unload the kitchen supplies and thought one of you ladies might guide us to settle them in the right places," he said.

"What do you think of our Claire?" I asked, feeling desperate and reckless at the same time.

Monroe's eyes held mine for a moment, then his gaze swept over Claire. "You look lovelier than the first day of spring," he said in sincere tones before bowing slightly.

"You're a vision, that's the truth," Arliss Edwards added.

Claire gifted them with a sad smile and an almost inaudible "Thank you."

"I'll help with the supplies," Victoria offered, interrupting the awkward silence, which had fallen after the forced compliments. The men, looking eager to leave, turned, and with Victoria following, made their way out to the kitchen.

"You do look lovely," I said, after the room had emptied.

"Thank you," Claire answered but still seemed troubled. She gazed down at the waterfall of creamy, almost white material then ran her hands reverently along the front of the dress. "It's finally finished," she said, her voice nearly a whisper.

"Yes."

"What are we to do now?"

As I gazed at my sister, a profound wave of affection filled me. I wished with all my heart that I could spare her any pain and disappointment our limited future might bring. I also wished I had more than one choice to offer when it came to saving her. Unfortunately, my wishes had been falling by the wayside for so long, I had little hope to sustain them. What I could give her was the truth.

"I intend to speak to Monroe about a marriage," I said, the words uttered out loud for the first time between us.

"I had thought as much," she said with a sigh.

"I know this is not what you had in mind when we began, but I hope you see it's the best course for us all. Monroe can give you a future. He can even take you to Savannah as you have wanted . . . although, as his wife." She gazed at me without anger or excitement. "Victoria, James, and I will be able to remain on Oak Creek and rebuild our legacy — your legacy as well."

My first well-spoken lie tasted like acid on my tongue.

"Could you not come to Savannah with us?" she asked. There were no tears, but her nervous hands twisted together at her waist betrayed her young age.

I couldn't bear to tear down every one of her dreams at once. "I'll do my best to find a way. But, you know" — I smiled the best smile I could muster — "husbands and wives rarely take relatives on their wedding trip."

She was not amused but seemed resigned. I accepted that and proceeded forward. "Let's get you out of this and hang it with the lavender sachet we made last summer. Better to serve a wedding dress than the linen closet."

As Victoria and I prepared supper, she listed the many supplies Monroe had purchased for our benefit, including a fresh twenty-pound sack of flour and three pounds of coffee beans. In our reduced position, we both agreed the continued bounty flowing from Monroe's goodwill seemed like a genuine miracle. Then, however, she dropped the fly into the honey pot. My sister always had a penchant for saving the bad news until last, perhaps to mitigate the worry.

"He said he received a letter from his mother today," Vee reported.

I felt as though my heart had fled my chest and taken up residence somewhere near my shoes. "Did he mention any news?"

Vee looked at me gravely and shook her head. "He said he hadn't had a calm moment to sit and read."

Time had run out.

After the supper dishes had been cleared and washed, I excused myself and went to my room to freshen up. I needed every ounce of courage for what I was about to undertake, and for a woman, much of her courage depended upon presentation.

I brushed my hair until it crackled around my shoulders and sparkled in the candle-light, then repinned it. I stripped down to my underclothes and suffered through a cold but bracing sponge bath before dressing in a fresh skirt and bodice. I spent my thoughts on the routine things so that I might control the shaking of my hands.

When I had run out of routine and was fully clothed, I sat down to gather my words to make sure they would match my intent. Surveying myself in the mirror, I looked perfectly calm, perfectly in control of my faculties. I only hoped I could present the same image to Monroe as I requested, or pleaded for, if it came to that, his help. For one brief moment, I closed my eyes and thought of William, touching his ring under the layers of my false courage.

"Please help me say the right words," I begged in a whisper. "You knew him better than I and must know what would sway him. Give me courage."

I left by the back door, hoping I wouldn't have to enter the men's sleeping quarters to conduct my mission. But, as with most other nights, Monroe and Arliss Edwards had built a fire on the lee side of the barn and were relaxing as men were wont to do. As I approached this camplike place I wondered for the first time if Monroe wasn't more comfortable outside by a fire than he would ever be in a house, especially a house in the city. He was leaning with his back and, with one leg bent, the sole of his boot against an over-hanging oak, whittling. Judging by the question he'd just asked Mr. Edwards, it sounded as though he was learning to carve wood from the alleged woodworker.

Feeling like an intruder on the private lives of these two men who'd helped us so much, I nevertheless pushed forward until I was inside the circle of light from the fire.

"Good evening," I said, speaking like I'd been invited into their solitude. Both men looked up in a surprised manner but remained where they were.

"Ma'am . . ." Mr. Edwards said, touching his hat in deference.

"Julia," Monroe said in response.

I swallowed and folded my hands together in front of me so as to appear calm. Now that the moment was upon me, I felt all my years of experience melt away. I fervently wished that my parents were here to handle such a delicate and important negotiation. My only thought centered on how proud we would be to include Monroe in our family, to call him brother.

"Monroe, I —" My voice deserted me in my need. I had to clear my throat and begin again. "I would speak to you privately for a moment."

He remained so still, I wondered if I'd

actually spoken or merely imagined the words. In contrast to Monroe's lack of action, however, Arliss Edwards rose to his feet.

"I think I'll go to my rest," Mr. Edwards said, then quietly replaced the tools he'd been using back into a rolled bundle. He touched his hat again before leaving. "Night ma'am."

"Good night, Mr. Edwards."

Never removing his gaze from me, Monroe pushed away from the tree and met me near the fire. Indicating a fair-sized log he and Mr. Edwards must have dragged into service for a place to sit, he asked, "Would you care to sit?"

I had no idea if he'd seen the look of near terror on my face, or not. I could feel my knees quaking under my skirts, however, and decided to accept the offer of a seat. I nodded and settled myself on the log. Monroe placed his whittling knife and plank of wood aside and sat next to me.

"Is something amiss?" he asked.

I couldn't just blather out my purpose without some decent interval of conversation. So, seeing the edge of an envelope, most likely the letter Vee had mentioned, resting in the side pocket of his coat, I thought to begin there. "I heard you've had some news from home . . ."

Monroe ducked his head, his gaze shifting away for a moment. "Why, yes, I have. My mother sends her good wishes to you and your sisters."

"Please thank her for me and return the sentiments."

He nodded but refrained from enlightening me further. "So, all is well with your family?" I continued.

"Yes. My father and brother despair of ever getting their business running normally again between the shortage of cash in the city and the meddling of Federal officials. I don't envy them the task. I've had a bellyful of the army chain of supply and command. One is always complaining to the other. I don't suppose that has changed with victory and the end of the war."

"You're a civilian now," I said, to what purpose I wasn't sure. Perhaps to remind him of his freedom to do as he wished.

He sighed. "Yes ma'am, I am. And I suppose I must do as my mother suggests and act like one."

"She wishes for you to come home," I ventured.

He didn't dispute me. "She asks if I've concluded the business which brought me here. She wonders why I've stayed so long."

I knew that he had done both. In fact, he'd gone beyond the limits even he must have determined. And here I sat next to him, ready to ask more. I drew in a breath and voiced the question before I lost my nerve and the opportunity. "I would ask one more thing of you."

As he waited, I watched the reflection of the fire in his eyes. He had an unusual expression, unlike any I could remember and I had certainly seen him in a variety of situations. I wished briefly that I could read his thoughts but then relinquished that hope. After all, he might not be thinking anything which would make what I had to say easier.

"I —"

Unable to control myself, I looked away from his discerning gaze and down toward the buttons of his vest. "I would ask that you consider marrying my younger sister, Claire, and taking her back to Savannah with you. You and I know that her intended will not be returning."

There, I had it out, part truth, part lie. In the heavy silence that followed my proclamation, I watched his chest rise and fall, the brass buttons glinting warmly from the flames. Then suddenly a branch cracked in the fire sending a shower of sparks upward.

I found myself gazing at Monroe's serious face once more.

He almost looked angry, and my pulse fluttered in anticipation of a rebuke for ungratefulness or worse, deceit. A man like him wouldn't have much use or patience for either.

"I'm sorry," he said, his voice sounding forced and unnatural. "I cannot marry your Claire."

"But —" I found myself reaching for his hand. "She's young and pretty. She'd make a fine wife and —" Words failed me and I felt my eyes filling with tears. How could I convince him when he'd never wavered or given me cause for hope? "You said your heart was still your own to give," I finished, nearly panicked.

His hand closed around mine and squeezed. "That it is."

When he didn't continue, I sniffed back my disappointment and readied another charge. He'd yet to fail us and I was certain that if I could find the right words . . . "Won't you at least speak with her, try to see if —"

"Julia." He stopped me.

With my one free, shaking hand I rubbed away the streaks of wetness on my cheeks. I hadn't intended to use tears as an advantage and refused to do so now. I raised my chin and waited for his declaration.

"In truth, there is only one woman on Oak Creek I would marry."

My heart labored in my chest as I sorted through his words. He couldn't marry Victoria, her James had returned. He wouldn't marry Claire. That left . . .

"You, Julia."

"But that's not possible!" I said, feeling like he'd pronounced the sky red, white, and blue instead of indigo with a scattering of stars.

He gazed down at my hand resting in his. "I understand that," he said in a low voice. Feeling shocked and too jittery to make any sense, I nervously pulled my hand away. I felt like he'd changed in front of my eyes and become someone totally different than I'd expected, than the man I'd grown to depend on. Not brotherly at all.

"It's not possible," I mumbled less forcefully. I had no idea what else to say. Marriage for myself had never entered my mind, and certainly not to Monroe. He'd been William's friend — *Oh, William.*

When he met my eyes again, he seemed ten years older, sadder, like the war had caught up with him after six months of giddy freedom. "Then you'll understand that I cannot remain here much longer. It's time for me to get on with what's left of my life. My own family needs my help."

I swallowed to ease the phantom lump in my throat that threatened to cut off my breath and nodded. All was lost, Claire's future, Monroe . . .

"Good night, Julia," he said then stood and walked away into the darkness.

I sat for quite awhile as the fire burned down, unable to think of what to do. Everything around me was in a shambles, and I could not shake the conviction that it was somehow all my fault. I'd sworn to myself and my sisters that I would do anything to convince Monroe to marry Claire. But he wouldn't marry Claire, because of me.

The confusion of it hurt my head. In the beginning of this wedding dress venture I had worried that I might have gone around the bend. For a moment, there alone in the darkness, I envied those who truly had given up and lost their minds.

At least their rambling questions didn't require answers. Then I remembered that Victoria was waiting for news. And as had been the trend at Oak Creek in the last few years, the news would be bad. Slowly, I pushed to my feet and went to spread the doom.

"Are we to have a spring wedding then?" Victoria asked, her excitement showing in the fact that she had accosted me just inside the kitchen door before I'd made it into the house proper. It was as good a place as any to say what must be said. The stove kept that room warmer than the rest of the house and Victoria had lit a lamp. I shrugged off my cape and sat down heavily in the ladder-back chair near the door.

"What's wrong? You look so pale," she questioned when I didn't answer. "Did you see another ghost?" She took my cold hands and chafed them.

Perhaps I'd seen the ghost of my life, I thought. The pale remnants of marriage and a husband . . . the future.

"Monroe won't marry Claire," I said.

Victoria seemed truly surprised. "What do you mean? The dress is finished, he must marry Claire."

I almost laughed at her unwavering certainty in our power to spin a wedding out of air and a dress. But, what I knew I had to say next took away any desire for levity. I pulled my hands from hers.

"He said the only woman he would marry would be me." I waited for Vee's amazement at that, or her indignation.

Instead she laughed.

And laughed.

As a matter of fact, she couldn't seem to stop laughing.

My indignation rose instead. "And what do you consider so funny?"

She pressed a hand to her chest, made her way to the chair opposite mine and gasped in a few breaths. She seemed to be doing her best to get under control. But, she was still smiling when she finally managed to speak. "That's wonderful!"

"Wonderful? I'm afraid I don't see your point."

"You and Monroe. I'm astonished you hadn't realized it before."

"Sister," I warned, growing testier by the moment. "Stop your dithering and tell me what you mean."

"He has from the beginning always looked to you. I thought it was his promise to William, but it's beyond that. You've stolen his heart."

"I have done no such thing!" I protested. "The idea!"

"Julia." Victoria calmed her gaiety and faced me with a long-suffering sigh. "I am not accusing you. I'm trying to make you see."

I was beyond placating. "See what?"

"That you and Monroe might do very well together. He and Claire never —"

"He has never made an effort where Claire is concerned," I explained.

"I rest my case," Victoria said and folded her hands on her skirts as though she'd settled the matter.

"He doesn't care for me. He only feels a responsibility for me since William saved his life."

She nodded. "And he has done his best to fulfill his so-called responsibility. Anything beyond this point will be settled between you and him."

"There can be nothing, as you say, beyond this point. I cannot marry a man simply because he says so."

Victoria remained silent, leaving me enough rope to hang myself without her help.

"We — He doesn't even know me. We've never even been alone together — not in that way. How can he think I could forget William's memory so soon?"

"I see," Victoria said.

I felt the rope tightening around my throat. "You see what?"

"It's William's memory that is the important issue here."

"You say that like it shouldn't be."

Again, she held her tongue and watched me. My nerves forced me from my seat. Determined to gain control, I stood and walked to the stove and, as if it needed stoking, I opened the fire door and added a few twigs.

"You have no feelings for Monroe then?" Victoria asked.

At her mention of feelings, my mind sifted back through the memories of Monroe that I held inside. I remembered his kindness with Claire, his clever solution to dancing with three spinster sisters without slighting any. I remembered the evening he'd told me William must have sent the spirits and then his words, *"I know if I were on the other side, I would send whomever I could."*

Monroe had touched my heart in many ways. I could barely envision a future without him in our lives. But I had thought of him as a brother, not as a . . .

"My feelings are of gratitude and the hope he'd be our brother soon by his marriage to Claire," I said, although I knew there was more to it than that. He had helped me personally on many occasions with no further prompting than his understanding that I needed his help.

Victoria watched me as my mother used

to do when she'd decided I hadn't told the entire truth. It was discomforting. I charged onward. "I cannot imagine anything beyond that."

Looking disappointed, Victoria nevertheless nodded. "We must set him on his way then."

Her declaration made the room seem colder. "What do you mean?"

She stood and brushed her hands together. "I mean, we have no cause to delay him further. We should thank him for the wonderful friend he has been and send him back to his family. We have no claim to his attention."

"But what about Claire?"

"Claire will fare as the rest of us do. We'll manage."

"Perhaps if you talked to him —"

Victoria stared me straight in the eye. "He has declared his heart, we cannot hope to change that."

"But he can't love me," I nearly wailed in frustration.

Victoria had started to turn away, but stopped. "And why would you think that, Julia? Are you not worthy of love?"

I felt trapped. "Well, I suppose. William loved me but —"

"And we, you and I have had our opportunities, is that the case?"

"Well, yes, and I'm not ready. I don't know how to start again."

"We all must start again, sister. There is no going back, and you yourself said we cannot cling to the past."

I had run out of argument, and it seemed my sister had run out of words. She made her way to the door, which led to the dining room, but before going through she spoke one more time.

"Decide if you can let Monroe go, if he's not worthy of your love now that William is no more. If not love, then a loving respect. And I don't mean for you to sacrifice yourself to save Oak Creek or the rest of us. He deserves better — you both do. If you can allow him to leave here without a twinge of regret, then let him, and I will never mention his name again."

Chapter Sixteen

"I've decided I'd best be leaving tomorrow," Arliss Edwards, looking sad but determined, announced at the breakfast table the next morning. We had finished eating and were lingering over the pleasure of real coffee rather than a poor substitute.

The news was not unexpected, but still, when faced with a firm decision rather than a possibility, one needed a moment to adjust. All eyes shifted to James as we waited for his reaction.

"I understand," James replied with a nod. "I appreciate you staying this long." He seemed, if not happy, then resolved.

I myself had barely gotten past the shock of Monroe's declaration the night before, so Mr. Edwards's news made barely a ripple in my attention. Other than to wish me a good morning, Monroe had not spoken to me directly or acted as if anything out of the ordinary had occurred between us. A part of me was grateful for that, but another part of me wanted to take him to task for surprising me, for upsetting the perfect solution to our plans for Claire.

It was childish, really. And ungrateful. But, that is how I felt. Now that he'd declared himself, I spent all my time looking at him in this different light as though he was a new puzzle for me to solve. When in every sense he acted and appeared to be exactly the same.

"I've been thinking about it and decided you might as well take Samson with you when you go," Monroe said. "I'll be leaving here myself soon and don't have any need for him." His eyes met mine briefly then moved on. "I don't believe he'll be of much help to the ladies, and dragging him back to the man who sold him to me, although tempting, would, I fear, not be worth the trouble."

Leaving here soon. The words invaded my mind, making me feel hollow inside even though I'd just eaten a decent breakfast. There didn't seem to be one iota of regret in Monroe, however. Perhaps he'd be glad to be rid of us and our scheming. Perhaps his feelings didn't run deep enough to cause distress. He seemed more worried about Arliss and his mule than about matters of the heart.

"Why, you could sell him, Mr. Monroe. He'd bring a price."

Monroe gave Mr. Edwards a rueful smile. "I thought of doing just that when I first got here. That or shootin' him. But now, since he's proved himself willin' to work for you, you might as well have him."

"I could send you the money for him later, when I get set up."

Monroe nodded. "You can do that if you want to."

"You'll have to let us know how you fare in North Carolina, Mr. Edwards," Victoria said. "We hope you find your family well. I'm sure they'll be happy to have you home again."

"Yes ma'am. I hope to get my business going and settle down."

"Well, we're grateful for all you've done for James," Victoria added then slipped her hand over her husband's. Out of old habit, he turned his palm upward and folded his fingers around hers.

"You're welcome, ma'am."

The room fell to silence, and soon with murmured excuses and the scraping of chairs, the men left the table. Victoria, Claire, and I cleared the dishes, and I washed, doing my best to fill the time and put off the inevitable — my confession to

Claire about why she wouldn't be wearing her wedding dress in the spring.

When it couldn't be delayed any longer, Victoria and I invited Claire into the sitting room. She looked like a woman condemned to the gallows, and I didn't have the heart to drag out the sharing of the news.

"You won't be marrying Monroe," I said as soon as we were all seated.

A variety of expressions crossed my sister Claire's features. The first, surprise, followed by relief, then genuine confusion. "Why?"

Victoria sat back in her chair and left the explaining to me.

"It seems —" I had to clear my throat and begin again. "It appears his heart lies elsewhere."

Claire's expression cleared. "Well, that's as it should be. He should marry the one he loves. Is it someone back in Savannah?"

An innocent enough question, and one I might have expected given Claire's recent conviction that Savannah was the center of the known world.

"Well, no —"

"Monroe wishes to marry our Julia," Victoria announced.

"That's wonderful!" Claire exclaimed,

bringing her hands together in excitement. "I'm so happy for you!"

For a moment I thought she'd found the perfect return payment for the way we'd done our best to orchestrate her future, but when I looked in her eyes I could see true happiness. She thought I would be happy.

"Thank you, but I —"

"Our Julia doesn't want to marry Monroe," Victoria informed her.

Suddenly we found ourselves back in a state of confusion.

"But, why?" Claire asked.

Now, I could see the crevasse looming before me. How was I to explain to Claire that I couldn't marry a man I barely knew, a man I hadn't spent enough time with to develop any true feelings for, when I had recently expected her to do that very thing?

"I, ah —" This time I waited for Victoria to finish my sentence so of course, being perverse, she did not.

"My heart still belongs to William," I answered truthfully. "I'm not ready to marry again so soon."

"It's been over two years," Claire said, sounding older than her age.

"Usually a year is required mourning," Victoria added helpfully.

With both of them staring at me, waiting for an explanation, I felt trapped. "I didn't say I wouldn't consider it," I said, my voice a little sharper than required.

A slight smile of triumph played across Victoria's lips.

"Let's try the dress on you," Claire said, pushing out of her chair. "I bet it will fit. You and I are of a size." She practically danced across the room to take both my hands in hers. "After the wedding, we can all go to Savannah together."

After Claire left the room on the errand of retrieving the wedding dress, I faced Victoria once more. "What am I to do?"

For the first time since we'd entered the room she lost her amusement at my dilemma. "I think you should take some time to gauge your true heart on the matter. You should also talk to Monroe, and quickly, before he decides to leave us."

The vision of me seriously discussing marriage with Monroe made my head swim. What on earth would I tell him? And what would he think about the whole process? It was impossible. I wasn't ready, I hadn't a coherent thought in my head. And my heart, my heart . . .

I closed my eyes. *Oh, William. What am I to do?*

"You don't have to rush out there and tell him yes. Just tell him the truth about how you feel, see what he says."

"I don't know how I feel," I confessed. "Other than surprised and confused."

"Then tell him that much, at least. Don't allow him to leave here thinking he wasn't good enough for you to consider."

That got my attention. "I never said he wasn't good enough. It's me, it's —"

"Tell him — not me."

Claire returned in a flurry with the dress over her arm. Soon, without helping, I found myself stepping out of my day dress and being buttoned into Claire's wedding dress. She'd been right, the fit was almost perfect, a bit snug in the chest and the tiniest shade short in length, otherwise, it could have been made for me. Victoria insisted on doing the alterations right away, just in case.

As I went up the stairs to dutifully look into the mirror, I felt a fraud. Then I remembered my dream of the bloody dress which had haunted me and I began to cry.

Oh, William.

That evening, making excuses, I went to my bed early just to be alone and gather my thoughts. Victoria deserted my room for Claire's in deference to my mood, and I was glad. I wanted time to get back to my former self, the one I'd grown accustomed to: middle sister, diplomat and protector, standing between the world and Oak Creek. William's widow. I had been resigned to greeting the world wearing those faces. Now I had an entirely different future to contemplate.

Without a marriage or some help from an untapped source, we would lose Oak Creek. But still, in my heart, I did not believe that a good enough reason to marry Monroe. The unfairness of it would surely spoil any chance we might have to be loving partners. Monroe was a good man, he deserved to be loved.

Loving.

My only experience of love resided in memories bound tightly around William. I had no idea how to let those go and open my heart to another. And if I managed to and failed, bringing a new heartbreak to add to the old, I wasn't certain I could survive the loss.

But I didn't want to lose Monroe's friendship either. He'd come to us on an errand of honor and stayed until we'd begun to include him in our future. The thought of never seeing him again or knowing how he fared in the world made a tight knot form in my stomach.

What was the answer?

I did my best to turn the question over to God, but I drifted to sleep frowning, not a portentous sign.

And then I dreamed of ghosts.

I was walking through an encampment of soldiers — Sesesch. How far in the past I could not tell, although it must have been early in the war because the men were well dressed in newer uniforms, less tattered and threadbare than they would be in a year or less. They also seemed to be in high spirits, as though they faced a sporting competition rather than a bloody conflagration. As I strolled by tents, and soldiers gathered around campfires, I heard boasts of bravery to come and laughter over some message from home. I even heard a snippet of a song sung in the distance to the accompaniment of a harmonica.

They all looked very real to me, young and fierce, unaware of their dark destiny, whereas I felt ghostly. My feet seemed to barely touch the ground, like a specter from the future flying over the past from a crow's-eye view. At one point I stopped to watch several officers playing cards on overturned crates near the opening of a lighted tent. None acknowledged my presence, confirming my suspicions of ghosthood.

I tried one more test, however. As another soldier approached me on my stroll, I stopped and spoke to him, "Could you tell me where to find Lt. William Lovejoy of the 24th?"

The man looked startled but could obviously see me. "Why, yes ma'am," he said. "Straight ahead about fifty yards. Look for the blue regimental flag."

I thanked him and walked, or floated on. My heart had begun to pound in anticipation and I wanted to run. Could I actually find William? Could I speak to him one more time? The line of tents seemed to go on forever. But then, at last, I reached the blue flag. In the distance I could see what must be the officers' tents set apart slightly from the others.

"William?" I called, hurrying forward.

The men busy with their own tasks paid no attention to my passing, and I made no attempt to look right or left. When I reached the tent he'd occupied, I knew with the surety of a dreamer, before calling out again, that William wasn't there. I ducked through the flap and went inside just to be sure. There were all his things on the opened portable writing desk: the silver ink pen and matching well my father had given him for Christmas, the stack of stationery I had packed in his bag before he left to assure he could write easily and often. I picked up the small leather case he'd carried in his uniform jacket rather than packing it, and opened it to reveal the daguerreotype we'd had taken for our wedding day.

My emotions forced me to sit down on the cot, which didn't exist in the future, but in this bright moment in the past, held the weight of my husband when he took his rest. I tried to remain calm, to concentrate and find him in my mind's eye, but I could not. I stared at the memento of our wedding willing him to return. But I knew, for whatever reason, he could not.

Leaving the case open on his desk so he might notice it when he did return, I left the tent. Stepping outside, I looked up at the stars overhead, the same stars he walked under as yet a living man, and fought my disappointment.

"William!"

I woke up calling his name with no help or answers to calm my heavy heart.

"Before I go, I wanted to talk to you ladies about a prop— proposition," Arliss Edwards said, stumbling briefly on the word.

I surveyed the somber faces of my sisters and James and Monroe on this, the day we would say good-bye to our friend, James's companion. "Certainly," I replied. "Why don't we all go into the sitting room?"

Monroe stood back as the others moved toward the hallway. Mr. Edwards hesitated as well. I, as usual, blundered forth. "That includes you, Monroe. We have come to depend on your presence."

His eyes met mine and for the first time I saw emotion. Whether surprise or pain he covered it quickly by nodding and indicating he would follow me. The entire short walk to the other side of the house I felt as though his gaze bore through me, searching for my heart.

Mr. Edwards gestured for all of us to sit, but he remained standing. When he had acquired our undivided attention, he nervously rolled the edge of his hat as he was wont to do, cleared his throat, and began. "I believe I told you my trade is furniture making. I 'prenticed for three years in Ohio and aim to build my own mill to make fine furniture." He glanced at Monroe. "I've been tellin' Mr. Monroe here, how you ladies have some of the finest hardwood on your land that I've seen. And he said it wouldn't be improper for me to ask you to consider — to think about maybe selling some of those trees to me. Now, I couldn't buy the trees outright —" he went on hurriedly. "I'd have to pay you out of the sales after I build the mill and make the furniture, but I believe I can make a little money at it, even in these hard times. People still need furniture," he declared. "Mr. Monroe said he might arrange for some of it to go to Savannah to his daddy's store."

"Does that mean you would be coming back to settle in these parts?" James asked in surprise.

"Well, yes sir. I have to go and find my family — make sure they're all well. But unless they need me bad, I'd just as soon be where the trees are. Besides," he looked down at his boots for a moment, "you folks have been fine to me, and in these times, all of us need to have friends."

Friends indeed, I concurred. We also needed any future source of income we could obtain. The conviction that Monroe had put Mr. Edwards up to asking made me want to weep. He was ever looking after us, even though I had insulted him dreadfully. I couldn't look him in the eye so I glanced around to gauge the feelings of Victoria and Claire. They both nodded yes.

"We think that's a fine idea, Mr. Edwards," I said, speaking for my sisters and myself. "This takes the gloom out of your leaving, and we can look forward to your return." I wanted to say, please hurry, so that we don't starve in the meantime but I held my tongue.

"I've also decided to leave Samson here for the time being. I'm grateful to Mr. Monroe for giving him to me, but I just can't go off with him when you ladies have no horse to hitch to the wagon. I had a talk with Samson and I think he'll do fine in the harness. I showed Miss Claire how to convince him."

Claire seemed amenable to that idea, so the handed-about mule became the temporary property of Oak Creek Plantation. Monroe just shook his head but didn't dispute the gift.

"Now I'd best be gettin' on the road," Arliss Edwards said.

"I've packed you some food." Victoria stood, ready to fetch it. "Although since you'll be on foot, I may have to rearrange the bundle."

"And I want you to have this," Claire said, holding out one clenched hand.

Mr. Edwards stuck out his large, open hand and Claire dropped her treasure into his palm. "It's a pond stone from the creek," she explained. "See? It has streaks of light in it. I've had it since I was small. It'll bring you luck," she said with a shy smile.

"Why thank you, Miss Claire," Mr. Edwards said, turning the stone over in his hand as one might handle a nugget of gold. His fingers closed over it and he gazed at Claire. "I'll keep it safe in my pocket from now on."

We followed Mr. Edwards and Monroe outside for the final good-byes. With Victoria fussing over the bulkiness of the food she'd packed, and James asking routes and plans, we were like a bunch of old hens clucking over a wayward chick. The only opinion missing was the mule's.

At last it was time to go. Mr. Edwards shook hands with Monroe. He smiled and said good-bye to each of us with our names. "Good-bye Miss Victoria. Good-bye Miss Julia. Good-bye Miss Claire." When he reached James, he took his hand in a hard grip. "You let these ladies look after you, Mr. James. They be better for you than me any day."

"You take good care of yourself, Arliss," James ordered in a subdued tone. "Come back when you can."

"I will, sir." Mr. Edwards nodded, released James's hand and strode off. We remained, watching and waving until he reached the main road and disappeared from our sight.

"I had intended to beg, borrow, or steal a horse for you ladies before I leave for Savannah," Monroe said. "And I'm still of a mind to do that. You know my backward progress with that mule. Even though he saved Mr. James," he added quickly.

I pretended that hearing him say he was leaving didn't bother me in the slightest. When in truth it trebled the sadness I was already feeling at Mr. Edwards's departure.

"I think Samson will work for us," Claire spoke up. "Mr. Edwards and I practiced on ways to get him to listen to me."

Monroe looked amused. "And what ways are those?"

"Well, it seems he didn't believe me when I gave him compliments," Claire explained. "So I tried reading. That appeared to go over his head, although some of the passages from the bible made his ears twitch."

"So, what worked?"

Claire awarded him a beatific smile. "Why, all I have to do is sing."

"Sing?" Monroe looked dumbstruck.

"He prefers love songs, but he also perked up to 'Dixie.' "

Monroe gave out one loud laugh before shaking his head. "Now, I've heard it all."

Even I couldn't resist a smile at the picture of Claire singing love songs to a mule in order for him to pull the wagon. It almost cleared my mind of troubles until Monroe turned to James.

"I have some things to discuss with you, Mr. James," he said, his face losing its transcendence.

"Certainly," James replied. "If you ladies will excuse us." He took Monroe's arm above the elbow. "Lead on."

James spent most of the day with Monroe. I saw them sitting on the log near the fire. Then, when I went out to feed the chickens, I saw them walking down by the creek. They seemed to have a lot to discuss of a sudden, and to me it looked obvious that this was one more preparation Monroe needed to make before leaving.

By suppertime my nerves were frayed to a frazzle, and I knew I must clear up matters between Monroe and myself. Whether I could accomplish it mattered little. Making the effort was the right thing to do.

I waited until the others had adjourned to their usual occupation of Claire's reading in the sitting room before following Monroe's path to his "camp" behind the barn. He was sitting on the log staring into the fire with his legs crossed at the ankle, stretched out before him.

"A penny for your thoughts," I offered.

"You would be gettin' the worse part of the deal," he answered, then smiled to ameliorate the words as he patted the log. "Pull up a seat."

I sat, close enough to be hospitable but far enough away so that I wouldn't give the wrong impression. I had not come to fling myself on his mercy. I'd come to apologize.

"I want to apologize for my unkind reaction to your declaration the other night. What came out of my mouth had more to do with surprise than with true feeling."

He merely watched me as one might study a skittish horse, unsure which way to jump to get out of the way.

"You mean too much to me — to all of us for me to hurt you in any way. At the very least you were a good friend to William, and my gratitude for that is boundless."

His face changed slightly, a wince if I were to make a guess. He shifted his gaze to the fire at our feet, the far-off "soldier" gaze returning.

"Your William used to tell stories about his home, his family — and you. They were so vivid and eloquent, it was as though they were my own memories, my own escape from the death and destruction around us." Monroe sighed and pushed at a log with his boot. "Once we were all gathered in the gloom, sittin' out another night too wet and muddy for sleep, when he brought out a packet of letters from you. He opened one that held a small square of cloth. It was lavender with sprigs of flowers on it."

Monroe gave a low laugh. "Something like that is downright shocking to soldiers who've only seen mud and blood, dust and corruption for months on end. But he passed it around, letting each of us, with our dirty hands, hold that cherished memento of home for a precious second before passing it on.

"Later, when we were on our own, him and me by the drowned-out fire, he lay there in the dark and talked about the bright day you must have mentioned in your letter. The day you were wearing the lavender dress, with sprigs of spring flowers."

I felt my face growing hot at the memory. And for a moment, the urge to cry settled in my throat. I wanted to cry for the men, most of whom didn't return, for William who'd shared our memories with them, and for the memory itself.

"He said it was springtime, and you and he had gone out riding, planning to join up with friends at the river for a picnic. The day had passed brilliantly, with everyone in a gay mood. But then a storm had blown up and the picnic was ruined. Laughing in the rain, he said he'd helped you on your horse and slapped its rump to move it out. Then he'd vaulted on his own stallion and raced after you."

Monroe's eyes crinkled at the corners, and he gazed at me as though he could re-capture the past in his mind. "But you didn't ride for home."

I had to look away. The memory of that glorious day was too personal, too sacred to hear it from Monroe's lips.

"Don't be angry, Julia. You know him well enough to know he didn't give up any of your secrets. He just said that after re-turning you home, soaked to the skin and blushing from hair to neckline, your father proclaimed then and there that a wedding would take place before he had to get out his pistol."

Monroe laughed again and shook his head, as he sat up. He chose a stick from the pile on the ground and used it to re-arrange the logs of the fire. "When I met you, I could still see you racing away on that horse."

Silence punctuated with the crack and hiss of the fire spun out between us. But then he continued, "Don't get me wrong. Although it did pain me to see your spirit and those of your sisters broken by this war, it's not pity I feel for you. In the be-ginning I thought to pay my debt to your husband, but as time went on, I simply felt at home here. Felt . . . needed. Any fond-ness beyond that has to be delegated to my lonely heart.

"Suffice it to say, I never met another man like your husband, or, heaven forgive me, another woman like yourself. In truth, I had no other choice. I loved you before I met you."

His declaration caused my heart to teeter treacherously, as one who steps too close to the brink of a high windswept place — full of joy in the view but fearful of the fall. I looked down at my hands and tried to gather my thoughts. "I don't know what to say."

"There's nothing more to say." He tossed the stick into the fire. "I just wanted you to know my heart before I left. I didn't want you to believe I would dishonor William's memory by confessing my feelings if they weren't deep and true."

William's memory. The crux of the problem. Both of us had loved William, and it seemed that neither knew how to get along with life after his leaving. I, however, had held his memory close to heart by depending on him even in his absence.

"Do you remember the evening we stood by the fence? And I asked you about the spirits?"

He nodded.

"You said that perhaps William had sent them to watch over us."

He gazed at me solemnly, waiting for my point.

"I was so thrilled, because that's how I feel, that William *is* watching over me, loving me still." It was my turn to look away. "I don't know how to let him go, to refuse his care, to admit the end of our loving connection."

"I understand, Julia, I do. And I never meant to presume anything beyond my eternal friendship. It's just that when you asked for my help with Claire I had to speak up."

I met his gaze. "You are a good man, Monroe. A loving and faithful friend. Any woman would be blessed to have your love."

A flush of color rose above the collar of his shirt but he remained silent.

"You deserve to marry someone without a grievous past, a gay and charming young lady who'll help you forget the tragedy of the war. Not one who would remind you of it each time you take her in your arms."

Monroe shook his head sadly. "I think you and I both know there's no forgettin' the war. On my dying day, whenever that comes, I expect your William and all the others to meet me on the other side. To clap me on the back and bid me welcome as one they left behind."

The tears which had threatened before, now flowed freely. I couldn't have spoken if my life depended on it.

"I expect I'll leave on Sunday, after church," he said. "If there's anything else you need from me before then, let me know."

I pressed my gloved hand to my trembling lips and nodded.

"Good night, Julia."

Chapter Seventeen

I told no one of my talk with Monroe, other than to say I had apologized and that we were on even footing once more. I also had to inform my sisters there would be no wedding or trip to Savannah. Claire took it better than I had expected, perhaps because she sensed the undercurrent of grief I was experiencing. Or perhaps she held out a slim hope that our cousins, the Langhorns, would have a change of heart and welcome us still.

Hope. That is what I seemed to have lost.

The only bright spot in the following days concerned Victoria and James. As far as I knew, they still had not come to the agreement to be actual husband and wife in the true sense. Then, on Friday afternoon as I took a long walk to be alone with my thoughts, which happened more frequently of late, I came upon them accidentally. The weather had warmed again slightly as we were nearly into March, and as I stepped through the trees on my circuitous route back home, I saw my sister and her husband standing together near the creek.

The image of the two of them made my heart swell. The late afternoon sun sparkled on the water like a thousand diamonds, and I pitied James who must hear the creek rushing by but not be able to see those diamonds reflected in his wife's eyes.

But then a miraculous thing happened. Of a sudden, James stopped talking and drew Victoria to him. He touched her face with both his hands, and the longing in his sightless gaze made my chest hurt.

And then he kissed her.

My tears fell as I was sure my sister's did. I saw her twine her sturdy arms around him and hold him close and I knew as he must now be certain that she would never give him up. Until death.

The pity in my heart faded. I was happy for them both, to have found each other again. Retreating into the trees, I did my best to become invisible lest I spoil such an intimate moment. But my steps were lighter. One of my sisters, at least, had received her heart's wish. I could thank God for that.

Saturday came too quickly. Even though

I felt I had settled accounts between Monroe and myself, I remained unsettled in my heart. It seemed the more I said, the more needed saying.

We did our best to put a happy countenance on his imminent departure with a lavish supper by our standards. We had smoked turkey, provided by Monroe himself, corn mush, and white beans. Victoria even opened a treasured, newly discovered jar of canned peaches for a cobbler — the jar having slipped off the shelf in the cellar sometime in the distant past and rolled under a cabinet in the corner where it remained hidden.

Monroe entertained us with stories of his family until we could tell he missed them. He even assured us he would talk his mother into making the trip to the "country" someday and would certainly bring her to Oak Creek to meet us. I couldn't dispute him, even though I knew these promises of his were fleeting. Here one moment, gone the next. Like himself. I held one surety in my heart after watching him bare his feelings; once he left, he would not be returning to Oak Creek.

After supper, we all retired to the sitting room. As Monroe built up a merry fire in the grate, Claire read to us from one of my father's favorite books about courageous sea captains. When Claire tired, Victoria took a turn at reciting some of the sonnets my mother had loved. James helped her when memory failed.

I had no heart for the entertainment, but I did feel the need to soak up the essence of companionship. The need to remain in the pleasant daydream that our lives would go on, here on Oak Creek in my mother's sitting room, with friendship, joy, and love.

If my parents had been looking down upon this scene, they would think we had never been happier, our laughter brighter, our worries further from our minds. But my heart felt broken anew, and the fear that I'd been holding back threatened to overwhelm my pleasant expression. I had no doubt that the others in the room were feeling the same in their hearts.

We would hold on to what we could and let the rest slip away.

When we had run out of ways to stave off the inevitable, we said our good nights with the plan of attending church in the morning, then bidding a final good-bye to Monroe after dinner.

Claire went upstairs first. Monroe, who had learned his way in the dark, left for the barn by the front door. I followed Victoria and James up the stairs, carrying the lamp. I waited outside Victoria's room as she guided her husband to a seat on the bed. When she returned for the lamp, she whispered, "I'll be sleeping in my own bed tonight, with James."

I could see her eyes clearly in the lamplight, lit with joy, yet her expression begged for understanding. I jostled the lamp when I hugged her.

"I'm happy for you, sister," was the sum of my eloquence. But I meant it.

As I lay in bed, hoping for sleep, my mind kept wandering back to Monroe. The finality of saying good-bye in the morning weighed heavier than I cared to admit. I remembered Victoria's words, *If you can allow him to leave here without a twinge of regret, then let him, and I'll never mention his name again.*

Regret. My life seemed to be one long string of could haves or should haves. But one thing I knew for certain — I am Mrs. William Lovejoy, and that is who I remain. My life's course had been set by the war and I would have to live out my years the best I could thereafter.

Monroe would find his way as well, I had no doubt. He'd proved himself a fine man and a good friend and I . . .

I would miss him.

I closed my eyes on my tears and slept.

Late in the night, the dream came again.

It is my wedding day, and William stands tall and handsome at my side proudly wearing his lieutenant's uniform of the 24th Virginia. My William . . . my husband looks fearsome and beautiful, so alive and in a fever to claim me as wife before going to war. The beloved vision of him breaks my heart because I know what comes next. I remember the weary path of this dream too well. What comes next is that as I stand there, in front of family and friends — half of Patrick County — on the happiest day of my life, I look down at my beautiful, heirloom wedding dress, the same gown my mother wore to pledge her life to my father and see that it is —

— not covered with blood. In fact, it is not my mother's gown at all, it is the wedding dress we'd made out of fanciful wishes for Claire.

Surprised and confused, I looked to William for explanation and he smiled, nearly making my heart stop with the beauty of it.

"Come, dance with me, Jules. One more time," he said as he extended a hand.

I placed my fingers in his. He felt warm and alive, and I thought my heart might burst from joy. Then we were dancing, his arms close about me, as the years of loneliness and heartache fell away. By some miraculous blessing, I could touch the rough weave of his uniform, smell the familiar aroma of shaving soap and leather. He felt warm and substantial, and I knew I'd received my heart's wish. My William had come home to me at last.

For minutes or hours, we danced in a place I did not recognize, a place neither here nor there. Surrounded by golden, glowing lanterns that appeared to float in the twilight, our steps kept time to music emanating from the honeysuckle-scented air around us. It was the fulfillment of every wistful fantasy I'd ever imagined, and I'd never been happier.

Somewhere inside me, I knew this must be a dream. But, I stubbornly clung to my hope.

"Am I dead?" I asked, perfectly content if it be so.

My husband eased me away from him in order to look into my eyes. He seemed to have grown older, a touch of gray in his hair at the temples. "No, my love. You live still."

I felt the crushing weight of grief tugging at my joy. I did not want to discuss or even think about our separation, yet I gave him a measure of my true feeling. "My living still, I believe, is the problem."

He laughed then. I had forgotten his laughter, because it had disappeared with the responsibilities of the army — the first casualty of the war. Gazing into his happy, lighthearted features I felt a pang of envy. He seemed to have lost all sorrow and care. Whereas I seemed perpetually mired.

"You have many things to do yet," he said, more fatherly than husbandly before spinning me into a turn.

"Will you stay with me and guide me?"

His humor disappeared. He halted the dance, yet left his arms around me while he gazed into my eyes. "No. I cannot. I have sent those I could. But it is past time for me to go."

He scrutinized my face as one might in order to complete a detailed portrait of memory in the mind.

"I knew when I sent him he would love you," he said finally.

Without having to ask, I recognized who he meant. "Monroe," I whispered aloud. Guilt mixed with my amazement. "You sent him to . . . love me?"

William nodded and smiled. "Yes, an honorable man for the woman I love. He'll look after you. I wish for you both to be happy."

I felt totally adrift, yet I perceived in that moment the part of me which loved Monroe, the part I'd been hiding from myself behind my memories. William could see it with his otherworldly eyes.

"Be happy," he said, his arms sliding away from me. He turned to look over his shoulder as though someone had called his name. I knew it was time for him to leave and I would have to let him go.

I held on to his hand for one more moment. "Will I ever see you again?"

His smile returned with blinding brilliance and as a parting gift, he let me see the love he held in his heart for me. "Oh, yes, Jules," he said. "We'll meet again. Never doubt it."

I woke up with a start. As I felt the remnants of the dream slide away, I knew a pang of sorrow in my joy. Sorrow at the realization that it was only a dream, even though it had felt as real as life itself. As though William had crossed the boundaries of life and death to give me his blessing. Confused once more, I closed my eyes on the morning and tried to return to that place, to the dance, to William. I clutched his ring in my hand but nothing happened.

Forced back to my lonely bed I opened my eyes and sighed. That's when I noticed a telltale brightness in the corner of the room near the door. I sat up and stared into William's unwavering smile. In waking, he seemed much like the other spirits I had seen — there, but not there. He raised a ghostly hand in farewell, then turned and walked through the wall.

Victoria and James were already downstairs when I raced through the kitchen on my way to the barn.

"Where are you going? What's wrong?" Victoria asked.

"I must speak to Monroe," I answered, as my hand settled on the door latch. "I must tell him the truth." I had the door halfway open when James spoke.

"Wait!"

His tone of voice halted me in my tracks although my errand was urgent.

He felt in his pocket and brought out a folded piece of notepaper. "He's gone. He left this for you."

Shock held me immobile. "He can't be gone . . ."

"He can and he is. He left before sunrise." James extended the note further in my direction.

I took it and read:

Dear Julia,

I'm sorry to admit that I'm a coward at saying farewell. Better I should just get the leaving over with. Please forgive me, and know that I feel blessed to have known you and your family. I hold all of you dear. And as for yourself, you are ever in my heart.

Monroe

Oh, and I will have someone return the horse. I would not rest knowing you were depending on that mule.

My high spirits fled. So, while I had been dancing with William, Monroe had taken himself out of my life.

"How long?" I asked James.

"I'd say probably an hour and a half," James answered.

I made up my mind before I could think of the twenty reasons I should just allow Monroe to go and be done with it. The main reason being that he might not appreciate a desperate, last minute reprieve, and I wasn't sure I could explain my change of heart without sounding crazy as a loon. I had to try, however, for both our sakes. "Vee, please wake Claire and send her to the barn. We have to get the mule in harness."

Victoria went through the door to the house. I stepped outside on my way to the barn.

Thirty minutes later, as Claire and I fastened the final buckles on the harness, Victoria and James came outside to check our progress. Claire led the mule into the traces while I explained my errand.

"You were right," I said to Victoria. "I cannot allow him to leave without regret. I do love him."

Vee smiled and hugged me. "Then you must bring him back, by any means."

"I will," I declared, although I knew much depended on Monroe's reaction.

James caught my hand up in his and squeezed. "He'll need more than luke-warm promises," he warned. "You must say the words, tell him all."

I hugged James. "I'll do my best."

Victoria pushed a sack of cold biscuits into my hands along with a sunbonnet and gloves as I boarded the wagon. Claire handed up the reins and with a last wave, I snapped the leather.

Nothing happened.

The mule looked half asleep and not inclined to move. I slapped the reins a second time against his hindquarters with a little more force. Jeremiah would have lumbered halfway down the drive by now.

The mule stood his ground and had the nerve to turn and look at me. I remembered Monroe's reluctance to have us depend on him. "Don't just stand there! Go!" I shouted in frustration. Raising my voice, however, seemed to make him more determined not to listen.

"You'll have to sing, Julia," Claire instructed.

"Sing?" I felt as though my entire future was slipping away and my sister wanted me to sing.

"He won't go unless you do," she added, then she began to sing the first verse of "Dixie," "Oh, I wish I was in the land of cotton . . ."

Victoria and James joined in. "Old times there are not forgotten . . ." I was the last to take up the refrain, "Look away, look away, look away, Dixieland . . ."

I snapped the reins, and lo and behold, the mule started forward. Then and there I decided if I had to sing all the way to the rail station at Danville, so be it. The others

326

continued to sing along until the mule and I turned onto the main road and were too far away to hear. Then it was up to me alone to maintain the serenade.

There's one thing about singing, while you're doing it you don't have the luxury to think or to worry. It was better than a two-and-a-half-hour trip to Danville from Oak Creek. I didn't want to think about the newly rebuilt railway that might, according to its new, efficient schedule of late, take Monroe on to Savannah before Samson and I could catch him. So, I kept singing.

Ten repetitions of "Dixie" had only gotten us a few miles down the road when I decided to try "The Yellow Rose of Texas." The mule seemed to approve of the change. He fell into a steady trot-walk while his ears bobbed back and forth like flags.

I'd grown nearly accustomed to the sound of my own voice before we met anyone on the road. The first carriage we met held a man and what must have been his wife — strangers. That made it easier for me to wave and stop singing long enough to call out a greeting as I went by. The man pulled up on his horse as though he might strike up a conversation, but I had to sing louder and pretend I didn't notice. I had the firm conviction that if I stopped, I might not get Samson moving again.

I met several more Sunday drivers before realizing that everyone must be on their way to church — where I would have been with Monroe if I'd had the sense God gave a flea and spoken up sooner. Since I was headed in the opposite direction from the Methodist church, and some of the people I passed would certainly recognize me and mention my strange behavior to Reverend Pembroke, I did the best I could to mitigate my circumstances.

I began singing hymns. Samson seemed particularly partial to "Nearer My God to Thee."

We were well over an hour into our journey, and had just passed the crossroads that led to Patrick City or Shelton, depending on which way you turned, when I heard a voice.

Or, I thought I heard a voice.

We were near the river so sounds seemed to echo. I kept going and switched back to "Dixie" in order to bolster my courage. I'd forgotten to bring Papa's pistol.

Then I heard it again.

"Hey!"

Without pulling up on Samson I turned on the seat. There was no one behind me, only the dust from our passage and the trees along the river. I thought of ghostly soldiers and wondered if they followed on our heels.

I started to turn back and hurry the mule when I saw a man step from the trees. This time I heard him loud and clear.

"Julia?"

It was Monroe.

I "whoa-ed" Samson and told him the news. "We've found him!" Before I could vault down from the wagon, Monroe was there to offer his hand.

"What in hades are you doing here? Has something happened?"

He looked as ever, the concerned friend wishing to help, and that raised my hopes.

"Yes, something has happened," I said, pausing to straighten my bonnet and smooth my dress. "I've had a dream I must tell you about."

Now I know most of you think I should have told him the dream of dancing with William and his blessing, but truth be told I wasn't ready to share such a private moment. Besides, I didn't think it fair to say I loved him because William gave his permission. As James had counseled, Monroe needed to know I'd come to the decision on my own.

So we sat by the river, and while the water eddied past as relentless as time, I told him of the dream I'd had about Oak Creek, about green fields and my mother's rose garden in bloom — about seeing him in shirtsleeves and suspenders and waving. I even confessed I'd thought at the time the dream concerned Claire, although he pointed out that my sister was absent from the picture. I told him I believed the roses meant love in bloom and that I'd come to realize, almost too late, that I did love him and wanted to be his wife if he would still have me.

"I will and I'm glad to hear that," Monroe said, his eyes sparkling from the light dancing on the river. "I was having a heck of a time getting to the rail station. I've stopped to rest my horse three times this morning, and he's as spry as a colt."

"Well, what of me? Having to sing to Samson for twenty miles."

Then Monroe's manner became more serious. He reached for my hand and handled it as though it held both our futures. "Are you sure, Julia? About you and me, I mean."

I laced my fingers into his. By whatever means and with William's help, I had abolished all my doubts. I was as certain in my love as I had ever been about anything in my life. "You told me once that I knew what love is about."

He nodded. "I did."

"Then don't doubt me now. I love you, Monroe Tacy. Not for what you have done for me but for the man that you are. Whither thou goest, I will go."

Monroe went completely still. I watched him swallow once before clearing his throat and nodding. "We're not going anywhere if I have to sing to that mule," he said, his mouth shifting into a smile.

"Just think, if you'd shot him that first day, we'd never have found each other again," I lectured.

A wonderful thing happened then, even more wonderful than finding Monroe before he left me.

He kissed me. And as his lips met mine, I knew I'd found home.

Chapter Eighteen

There was a wedding that spring at Oak Creek Plantation and half the county attended. The Satterwhites were there along with the Tates and even a few of the Peltons. There were only a few comments or questions concerning the bride and exactly which sister would be wearing the wedding dress. The controversy was soon settled, however, when Mrs. Julia Atwater Lovejoy, that would be me, exchanged vows to become Mrs. Monroe Tacy.

I stood beside Monroe before our friends and Reverend Pembroke, wearing the wedding dress my sisters and I had fashioned from our hopes and dreams and prayers. Before the ceremony, I'd made an addition to the lace and handwork we'd done by carefully sewing one of the fragile lace appliqués from our mother's dress onto the bodice. *Something old, something new.* I'd also removed William's ring, which I'd been accustomed to wearing around my neck, and placed it in my box of keepsakes. Dreams from the past would plague me no more.

The finishing touch to my bride's ensemble came in the form of shoes. Monroe, after informing his family about our upcoming marriage, asked his mother to send me a pair of shoes worthy of his bride. We'd expected them to arrive by mail and waited impatiently. Instead, Monroe's mother herself delivered them along with his father and one younger brother.

"After all," she'd said, "we knew you'd hold up the service for us since the bride would have to walk down the aisle barefoot otherwise."

Little did she know, but I would have done just that. Once an Atwater makes up her mind, there's no stopping her. And all of the Atwaters pledged together on one course are a veritable force to be reckoned with.

The wedding dress had one more bit of magic to perform for me it seemed. When Reverend Pembroke called for Monroe to place a ring on my finger, he produced a gold band he'd purchased from Mr. Tate in town — it was my very own ring I had sold before he'd arrived in my life. The circle had been completed.

Oak Creek Plantation had come alive again, with a future and with hope. In the making of the wedding dress my sisters and I had somehow brought James home to us, and now Monroe. Even Claire would have her wish to travel to Savannah since we would be returning there on our bridal trip. I could not speak for the others, but my faith had been restored along with my life and home and heart.

I believe the spirit world rejoiced along with us. When the wedding was over and we were all, Monroe's family, Claire, and the newlyweds, packed to leave, I waved good-bye to Victoria and James. Mounted on one of my wedding presents, a sturdy-legged mare named Guenevere, I rode alongside my husband at a distance behind the carriage. Then out of sheer exuberance I challenged him to a race, giving my mare her head before he'd had the opportunity to accept the challenge properly. Flying down the drive past the wagons, with Monroe closing the distance between us, I nearly missed the sight of those we'd become accustomed to.

At the end of the drive, one on either side of the gate marking the entrance to Oak Creek, were two ghostly soldiers. The one on the left looked particularly like my

William. They came to attention as I raced by, smiling into the wind. I glanced back over my shoulder and saw Monroe raise his hand in a salute as he passed them. By the time I pulled up and turned Guenevere, they had both disappeared.

Epilogue

October, 1870

Patient listener, I cannot end the melody of our story without a few lingering notes . . .

Oak Creek is graced with children again. Monroe and I have a son, William, and a daughter named Amelia to brighten our days. My sister Victoria also has a daughter named Charlotte after Charlotte Brontë, who is her daddy's pride and joy and his new purpose in life. James spends a good bit of time reciting silly poems or serious verse to her and insists his daughter will grow up to be a famous literary talent like her namesake. James has also taken it upon himself, with the help of a sighted assistant, the task of teaching many of the children from the surrounding farms to read. In his esteemed opinion, there is no excuse for overlooking ignorance, even blindness, and he expounds on the subject anytime there is an administrator, church elder, or

336

politician within twenty feet. We would not be a bit surprised if he argues his way to the state house.

Speaking of politicians, the state of Virginia has recently been readmitted to the Union, yet all is not perfect in our world. We've had lean times and struggle with this new system of government under reconstruction, but we survive. Our crops are plentiful, and Monroe has taken to growing tobacco, which brings a good market price no matter what his political affiliation.

I have refurbished my mother's rose garden with some treasured cuttings given to me by Monroe's mother. They are English roses and add a lovely scented accent to the tried-and-true bushes my mother loved. Much like Monroe gave his heart and hands to me and to Oak Creek, and our family has flourished.

In terms of our extended family, Arliss Edwards did return to us and runs the mill in partnership with his brother Luther, Monroe, and Samson the mule. Mr. Edwards's craftsmanship is well known in the county. His furniture has made our trees famous and is much in demand. It seems the lot of us have found our homes again.

As a final note I must mention that another wedding took place this past spring. Miss Claire Atwater married Mr. Regan Conners of Savannah in a small service attended by both families. To my great delight, the Langhorn relatives who attended were scandalized when Claire insisted on wearing a homemade wedding dress of buff calico. The work of our hands, of our prayers, and our dreams, the wedding dress had come full circle. It had fulfilled its promise to us and we had fulfilled our promises to each other. Our Claire simply announced that the dress was sure to bring her good fortune.

Victoria and I wholeheartedly agreed.